F

S.

W

P

T

**Nick stood before her. He held open his arms, and she ran to him.**

While they blocked the elevator door to keep it from closing, she kissed him for all she was worth. "We have to go."

"Not you," he said. "I'm the one they want. I want you to go into the back of these offices and put your head down."

"What's going to happen?"

"Not much, I hope. I got all the explosives detonated, except for the one in my uncle's office. I had it all set up to rappel down the side of the building, but there wasn't enough time."

"When the bomb goes off, what happens?"

"It's not in the right place to take down the building. There's going to be damage on the ninth floor."

"Where the hostages are," she said.

The elevator dinged madly. "If they keep their heads down, they'll be okay."

"Let me come with you."

He stepped into the elevator. "Stay safe. We'll be together."

She watched the door close and could only hope that wasn't the last time she'd see him.

# Hostage Midwife
# CASSIE MILES

To Fifi and Isis. And, as always, to Rick.

First published in Great Britain 2013
by Mills & Boon, an imprint of Harlequin (UK) Limited.
Large Print edition 2013
Harlequin (UK) Limited,
Eton House, 18-24 Paradise Road,
Richmond, Surrey TW9 1SR

© Kay Bergstrom 2013

ISBN: 978 0 263 23816 7

Harlequin (UK) policy is to use papers that are natural,
renewable and recyclable products and made from
wood grown in sustainable forests. The logging
and manufacturing process conform to the legal
environmental regulations of the country of origin.

Printed and bound in Great Britain
by CPI Antony Rowe, Chippenham, Wiltshire

## CASSIE MILES

Though born in Chicago and raised in L.A., *USA TODAY* bestselling author Cassie Miles has lived in Colorado long enough to be considered a semi-native. The first home she owned was a log cabin in the mountains overlooking Elk Creek, with a thirty-mile commute to her work at the *Denver Post*.

After raising two daughters and cooking tons of macaroni and cheese for her family, Cassie is trying to be more adventurous in her culinary efforts. Ceviche, anyone? She's discovered that almost anything tastes better with wine. When she's not plotting Mills & Boon® Intrigue books, Cassie likes to hang out at the Denver Botanical Gardens near her high-rise home.

# Chapter One

*Sunday, 9:57 p.m.*

The electricity to the building had been cut, but the emergency lights were enough for Kelly Evans to see as she moved toward the exit sign on the sixth floor. Her pulse raced and her hands trembled. Every step brought her closer to danger, but she didn't have a choice. She had to save the other hostages.

Carefully, she opened the door below the exit sign and held it ajar. When she closed the door, it would lock behind her, and there would be no escape from the stairwell.

Holding her breath, she listened. Had they

posted a guard in here? Was she walking into a trap? Smoke from the earlier explosion that closed off the stairwell at the ground floor tainted the air and irritated her throat. She pinched her lips together, stifling a cough that might betray her position.

She eased the door closed with an almost imperceptible click. Stepping away from the wall, she leaned forward, gripped the metal banister and peered upward. Each floor had a lighted exit sign, but the peripheral shadows created an optical illusion, making it appear that the winding flights of stairs disappeared into infinity like Jacob's ladder. Kelly started her climb.

Halfway between the seventh and eighth floors, she paused to catch her breath. The ninth floor was the most dangerous. Trask was there, and the men with the guns. If she got beyond that point, she could make it to the roof.

From below, she heard a door crash open. A rough male voice echoed against the concrete walls. "Is she in here?"

"Shut up and listen. If she's close, we'll hear her breathing."

*How long can I hold my breath?*

After a few impatient seconds, the first voice said, "I don't hear a damn thing."

"We're out of time. Head back to the ninth floor."

The soles of their boots scraped against the stairs as they climbed. They were coming toward her. She had to move…and to breathe. She gasped, quietly. On tiptoe, she tried to glide with perfect stealth from stair to stair—an impossible task. *Don't let them hear me, please, don't let them hear…*

She stumbled, catching herself with her hands.

From below, she heard a shout. "Hey, she's up there!"

Darting past the ninth floor, Kelly stayed as close to the wall as possible. Only one more floor…

"Do you see her?"

"Not yet."

Their voices sounded close. A burst of gunfire from an automatic rifle echoed against the
concrete walls.

She took the last flight of stairs two at a time.
At the roof, she hit the crash bar and dashed
outside into a cold, starry night. There was no
way to lock the door behind her. All she could
do was run.

Dodging around air vents and solar panels,
she crossed the roof and peered over the waist-
high parapet. The street below was filled with
dozens of emergency vehicles, their red-and-
blue lights flashing. This was the wrong side
of the building. She needed to be facing west,
toward the foothills. She ran to the corner of
the building, made the turn and found what she
was looking for.

Behind her shoulder, she heard the door open.
Gunfire erupted.

She climbed onto the parapet. Looking down,
she saw the roof of a four-story building far

below. She wasn't afraid of heights, but vertigo washed over her in a dizzying wave.

She crouched into position and went over the edge.

*One week earlier. Sunday, 6:07 p.m.*

FIVE VERY PREGNANT WOMEN in loose-fitting workout clothes sat in a semicircle on exercise mats facing Kelly Evans. Behind each lady was her mate, except for Lauren Spencer, who was unaccompanied. Lauren craned her neck and stared at the glass double doors leading into the gym.

"Typical," she muttered. "He's always late."

"It's okay," Kelly assured her. "You can fill your partner in on anything he misses. We should get started."

Kelly tried to keep her Lamaze classes convenient, non-threatening and on schedule. Each of the six sessions in this two-week period was supposed to be an hour and a half, and she'd do everything she could to honor that time commitment. If couples wanted to stay later, they were welcome to do so, but she knew these people had places to go and things to do, even on a Sunday night.

"Before we get into the exercises," she said, "I want to take a few minutes to introduce ourselves and give you a chance to ask questions."

"You start," Lauren said. "The rest of us have met before. Valiant is a pretty small town."

Clearly, Lauren was the leader of the pack. Not only was she nearly six feet tall and built like an Amazon, but she'd married into the Spencer family, which granted her instant status. From what Kelly knew about this town in the foothills between Boulder and Fort Collins, the Spencers were among the earliest residents. The main office for their property and construction business was based in Valiant. In fact, this class was taking place in one of the classrooms attached to the gym on the second floor of the Spencer building, a ten-story structure in a small office park.

"I'm a certified nurse-midwife," Kelly said. "I've been in practice for about three years in Austin, but I used to live in Denver. And I'm happy to be back in Colorado."

Actually, she was far happier than she'd expected. While driving here, her first glimpse of the Rockies had lifted her spirits and started her yodeling an impromptu concert of old John Denver songs. The dry air tasted fresh. The skies glowed with a brighter shade of blue. She couldn't think of why she'd ever moved. What was it again? Oh, yeah, the divorce.

When she'd left her husband five years ago, she'd gone back to nursing school in Texas. Though she and her ex never discussed location, he had taken custody of Colorado. It made sense. In addition to being a lawyer, he was a representative to the state legislature. With his new wife and baby in tow, he'd recently started making political moves toward running for national office. She hadn't contacted him but was sorely tempted to leave a phone message: "I'm ba-a-a-ack."

One of the women asked, "How did you meet Serena?"

"We've known each other for years and years. By the way, she sends her best wishes for you all." Serena Bellows, the local midwife, had called Kelly to fill in with her clients while she took a brief maternity leave. "I'm staying with her at the farm."

"With the llamas?"

"And the goats and the chickens and the horses and the mules," Kelly said with a grin. "And the children. I assisted with the birth of number four last week—a daughter who weighed in at nine pounds, three ounces. We used an underwater technique. Is anybody interested in that?"

There was a chorus of "no."

"Any other questions?"

A petite brunette with asymmetrical bangs said, "I love your blond highlights."

"Thanks." Kelly smoothed her straight brown bob with the sunny streaks around her face.

"I'm a stylist," the brunette said. "My shop is named after me—Roxanne. If you decide to stick around in Valiant, I'd love to do your hair."

"I appreciate the offer, Roxanne." Kelly transitioned from talking about herself, which was always a bit uncomfortable, to talking about her clients. "When's your due date?"

"Next week. March twenty-first, the first day of Aries, and I can't wait. My belly gets in the way when I'm cutting hair, and I've been avoiding the chemicals used in perms and dyes."

A fresh-faced young woman whose name was, appropriately, Daisy piped up, "From what I heard, you aren't even supposed to be in the same room with those chemicals."

"If you use gloves," Kelly said, "you should be safe. It's not recommended to color your hair when you're pregnant, but the amount of dye absorbed through the scalp is negligible."

"The smell nauseates me," Roxanne said.

"Whenever anybody gets a perm, I have to leave the shop, go next door to the café and have a cup of coffee."

"Caffeine," said Daisy with a shudder of horror. "That's another no-no."

"Yeah, yeah," said Roxanne. "I know I said coffee but I meant tea, herbal-freaking-tea. I can't wait to have this baby so I can get back to my espresso."

"You might want to hold off after the birth," Kelly advised. "When you're breast-feeding, the caffeine goes through you to the baby. Trust me, the last thing you want is a wide-awake infant."

After a few more minutes' discussion about the trials and tribulations of pregnancy, Kelly sensed that the men were growing restless. She switched the topic to teamwork and how they would be the coaches, helping their partners through childbirth. "We'll start with massage. Gentlemen, lie facedown on the mats."

The glass door to the gym swung open, framing a very tall, broad-shouldered man in a tuxedo. At a glance, she could tell that this wasn't a rental tux. His clothing was designer and definitely tailored to accommodate his height, which had to be at least six feet, four inches. His thick black hair was mussed, and he'd opened the collar on his pleated white shirt.

"About time," Lauren snapped.

Kelly bounced upright on her bare feet and greeted him with her hand outstretched. "Pleased to meet you."

"Nick Spencer." His giant paw engulfed her hand. "The pleasure is mine."

As if the tux wasn't enough to jump-start her libido, his smile was pure charm. His blue eyes were rimmed with the kind of thick black lashes that a woman would kill for. Kelly shouldn't be thinking what she was thinking. Nick Spencer was a married man.

"You haven't missed much," she said. "Take off your shoes and lie down on the mat."

"Yes, ma'am." His voice was a low rumble. "I guess you like to get right down to business."

His eye contact lasted a bit longer than necessary. If she hadn't known better, Kelly might have thought he was flirting with her. With his blond Amazon wife sitting right there? Did this guy have a death wish?

As she instructed the women in the class about how to massage their partners, she subtly used the men as dummies to illustrate the musculature of the back, spine and hips. When these women were in labor, it would be useful for them to specifically tell where it hurt.

Another benefit to this part of the exercises was that the men loved the attention. In the teamwork approach to childbirth, it was important for them to feel included. Just as she was about to tell the couples to switch positions, a thin blonde woman in a strictly tailored pantsuit opened the door a crack and peeked inside.

"Excuse me." Her voice was thin and angry. "Nick, I need to speak with you. Now, Nick."

As he headed toward the exit, he leaned close

to Kelly's ear and whispered, "Keep going. I'll be right back."

His warm breath on her neck sent a purely sensual shiver down her spine. With an inadvertent gasp, she fought to control the sensation. Nothing good could come from being attracted to a married man.

The men were now massaging the women, and Kelly took Nick's place to rub Lauren's back. As soon as she touched the knotted muscles and tendons near the neck, Lauren winced and groaned. She was carrying a lot of tension—not a surprise, given the way her husband behaved.

Through the glass doors leading from the gym, Kelly watched as he hugged the rigid-looking blonde. She quickly shoved him away. Though Kelly couldn't hear what they were saying, the blonde seemed to be chastising him—glaring and shaking her finger in his face.

"She's the company accountant," Lauren mumbled. "Marian Whitman has the reputation of being an ice princess—forty-two and never married. The only thing that arouses her is numbers."

Kelly didn't see it that way. Marian's cheeks were flushed, and her eyelashes fluttered as she looked up at Nick. Was this a personal conversation? Something strange was going on here.

As the class moved into another position, Nick rushed back through the door. Passing Kelly, he leaned close again and said, "Did you miss me?"

Okay, this was definite flirting, and she didn't like it. For the duration of the class, she kept her distance from him, ignoring the way he moved and the sexy timbre of his voice when he asked questions. She hid behind a mask of professionalism, suppressed her smiles and avoided friendly banter with him.

When the class was over and everyone else had left, Nick and Lauren approached her. "I'm really sorry I was late," he said. "I had to attend a charity benefit."

"The Spencer Academic Awards," Lauren said. "It's a scholarship program for Colorado students going to Colorado colleges. Since the Spencers made their fortune during the Colorado gold rush, we feel like we should give something back."

"The Spencers were gold prospectors? That's so interesting."

"Is it really?" Nick said drily.

"Family histories fascinate me." She tried not to look at him. "Especially when they deal with the Old West."

"It was 1862 when my ancestors hit one of the biggest gold strikes on the front range of the Rockies. Our mine, the Valiant Mine, was bigger than the Glory Hole near Central City."

Lauren patted her belly. "My baby is going to be born into an impressive family tradition. In this very building, on the ninth floor, we have fifty kilobars of gold from the Valiant Mine."

"Actual gold?" Kelly couldn't believe it. That much gold would be worth a small fortune.

"Processed and smelted right here in Colorado. Every bar is stamped with a *V* for *Valiant*." She beamed proudly. "Anyway, Nick has promised he wouldn't be late, and my *real* partner will be here for the session on Sunday night."

Kelly was confused. She was beginning to feel like Alice in Wonderland, talking to people who spoke only in riddles. "Excuse me, did you say your real partner?"

"My husband, Jared. He's out of town, wrapping up some important business in Singapore."

"So Nick isn't…"

"My husband?" She laughed. "No way would I marry this big ox. Nick is my brother-in-law."

He bent down to look directly into her eyes. At six feet four inches, he was probably a foot taller than she was. "Since you're interested in family history, I'd like to take you upstairs and show you my gold."

Embarrassed that she'd jumped to the wrong conclusion and regretful that she'd treated him coolly for most of the evening, Kelly dared to gaze directly into those gorgeous blue eyes. "That's quite a pick-up line."

"Did it work?"

*Indeed, it did.*

# Chapter Two

*Sunday, 7:43 p.m.*

Nick had been immediately attracted to Kelly. During the Lamaze class, she'd been barefoot, and he'd noticed that her toenails were painted in alternating shades of pink, yellow and purple. He'd imagined himself kissing those toes, running his hands up her long, slender legs, continuing up her body to her limber waist, onward to her breasts and finally her lips. That would be a trip worth taking.

While she lectured, he could tell that she was smart and had a sense of humor. And he was desperately seeking a diversion—a woman he could relax with and share a couple of laughs. His brain was on overload from dealing with the financial problems that plagued the family business.

"Just to make it clear," he said as he escorted her onto the elevator, "I'm not currently married."

"That implies that you once were married."

"I was," he admitted. "You?"

"Yes." She didn't look at him but faced forward, following elevator protocol. "In class, I might have been a little bit rude to you, but I'm not going to apologize. I thought you were Lauren's husband, and that you were hitting on me."

"Was I?"

"You were." Her voice was certain, but she fidgeted with the knot on the Kelly-green scarf she wore with her plaid jacket. "You stared at me. You whispered to me."

He ducked his head to put his lips close to her ear. "Maybe I was just being friendly."

"Friendly like a fox."

"What's that supposed to mean?"

"You don't look dangerous until you're ready to pounce."

"Scared?" he asked.

"I can handle a pounce."

"I bet you can."

Finally, she turned her head and looked at him. When her lips curled into a smile, her green eyes crinkled at the corners. He guessed she was in her early thirties, which was, in his opinion, the perfect age. They wouldn't have to waste time playing games.

"Tell me about the gold," she said. "Why do you keep it here instead of in a bank vault?"

"Spencer Enterprises is still family owned and operated, which means our company tolerates more than our share of eccentricity. My uncle, Samuel, is the last of the older generation of Spencers. He's kind of a genius when it comes to architecture. He designed this office park."

Forty years ago, the oil business had been

booming in Colorado, and Samuel had proposed a ten-story building and three others that were four stories each. There was a definite need for more office space in the Denver/Boulder area, but Valiant wasn't the most convenient location. Prevailing opinion—including that of Nick's father, who was the CEO—had been that good old Samuel had taken a swan dive into the crazy pool.

As it turned out, Samuel was right. Valiant was just close enough to Boulder and Fort Collins to be a viable corporate headquarters. They played up the outdoorsy lifestyle and the nearness to the mountains. When the oil and gas companies moved out, the software companies moved in. "Uncle Samuel situated Spencer Enterprises on the ninth and tenth floors. And he wanted the gold to be here."

"But why?" Kelly asked.

"Part of our corporate identity," he said with a shrug. "We do a lot of construction business all around the world. The clients who come here want to see the gold. They're usually impressed."

"How much is it worth?"

"Fifty kilobars at two pounds each." The elevator dinged at the ninth floor. "It's about two and a half million dollars."

She gave a low whistle. "That's a lot of money to leave lying around."

"We're eccentric, but we're not stupid. Our security is intense."

When the elevator door opened, Marian Whitman stood waiting for him. Though it was almost eight o'clock on a Sunday night, her grooming was sleek perfection. Not a single blond hair dared to slip out of place. The only color on her face came from her perfectly painted ruby lips. Her mouth barely moved when she said, "I expected you to be alone, Nick. We have business to discuss."

He didn't want to talk about corporate deficits and poor investment decisions. "It can wait."

"Your uncle is here. He's in his office. I think

this might be a good time to confront him, while there are no other distractions."

But Nick longed for distraction. He wanted to sling his arm around Kelly's slender waist and take her outside for a walk along the path outside the office park. He wanted to tease her and make her laugh while they looked up at the half-moon. The March air would be crisp and invigorating.

Kelly shook Marian's hand as she introduced herself. "I don't want to interrupt. I'll be going."

"Thank you," Marian said, "for understanding. Nick? Come with me."

Though she was the Chief Financial Officer and the undisputed queen of the corporate balance sheets, he was still the boss. "Here's what's going to happen," he said. "First, I'm going to show Kelly the gold. Then, I'll escort her downstairs to her car. If I'm lucky, she'll agree to come for a walk with me along the creek and we'll see a couple of chipmunks scampering away from the nighthawks. After that, Marian,

I'll come back here. Then, and only then, we can talk."

Not waiting for a response, he directed Kelly through the glass doors into the reception area for Spencer Enterprises. Behind his back, he heard Marian give an angry snarl. If he looked over his shoulder, he might see steam shooting out of her ears.

Kelly cleared her throat. "I wouldn't mind if we did this another time."

"I would," he muttered. "I spent the whole day dressed in a monkey suit, shaking hands and representing Spencer Enterprises. The last thing I want to do is spend my night mediating a rant between my uncle and Marian."

"Heavy is the head that wears the crown."

"Shakespeare?"

"Or somebody like that," she said.

He placed his hand at the small of her back and guided her around the receptionist's desk and into an open area with several windows on one side and cubicles for the accounting department on the other. "I suspect you've been around other people who thought they deserved to wear crowns."

"My ex was a lawyer. Lots of bigheaded people in that profession want tiaras and crowns."

As they strolled past the cubicles that were decorated with photos and personalized touches, the overhead lights—which were on motion sensors after the offices closed—came on automatically. Samuel had done an extensive upgrade on the electric and ventilation system in this building about five years ago. Though the decor featured saturated colors and lots of dark wood trim like an old-fashioned gentlemen's club, the underlying design was state-of-the-art.

The back wall of the ninth floor had a large office in each corner. "We're in front of Marian's office," he said. "On the opposite side, it's Uncle Samuel."

In the area between, Kelly paused to admire the gold-mining artifacts in two glass cases, including pans, winches and pickaxes. She studied the large oil painting above the oak wainscoting. The subject was a grizzled prospector leading a mule. She said, "That looks like a Remington."

"It's Remington's style, but my great-grandfather commissioned the painting from one of his contemporaries. The prospector's face is actually a portrait of Great-Grandpa Spencer himself. At one time, the ass had the face of his number-one competitor."

"Why was it changed?"

"After my great-grandpa drove the ass out of business, the painting seemed mean." He pushed open the door to a large conference room with a polished oak table, leather chairs and several other paintings hanging on the walls. "That little one with the bronco rider is a Remington."

"I like the historical touches. It's very Old West Colorado."

"Not really my taste," he confided as he crossed the room. "I like light and modern with clean lines. The office I usually work from is in the mountains."

"I thought you lived in Valiant."

"My brother wanted me to fill in while he was out of town for a week." His clever brother had also dragged him into the issues with Uncle Samuel. "I've got a condo here, but I live in Breckenridge. Most of my work is in the ski resorts."

At the back of the conference room, he paused beside a door that appeared to be dark oak. His knuckles flicked against the surface. "This entire section of wall and the door is heavy-duty steel."

"The security you were talking about." She came closer. "Is the gold in there?"

"This is only the first step." He flipped open a nearly invisible wall panel to reveal a keypad. After punching in a five-number code, he opened the door to a brightly lit room. The walls were lined with utilitarian shelves and file cabinets. "This is our secure area where we keep confidential paperwork, contracts and mapping information. We call it the vault."

"I'm surprised," she said. "I would have thought this information would be computerized."

"We're working on it. Some of these documents date back to the 1800s. If they ever got lost, we'd have a hard time replacing them." He took her by the shoulders and situated her in front of a floor-to-ceiling section of smoky gray glass that was about twelve feet long. "Ready?"

"Amaze me," she said.

He hit a switch and a light came on behind the glass, turning it transparent. Behind a wall of reinforced steel bars, the Valiant gold shone with a radiance that rivaled the sun. The stacks of fifty kilobars took up about as much space as a medium-size coffee table. Nick had seen the gold hundreds of times. He'd held the kilobars and felt their weight in his hands. Still, being this close always gave him a thrill.

Kelly whispered, "Can I touch it?"

"Afraid not."

She leaned forward, almost pressing her nose against the glass wall. "I don't think I've ever experienced the real color of gold before. It almost seems alive."

He heard the excitement in her voice as she continued. "When I look at this, I can understand why gold has been coveted throughout history—from King Midas to the search for El Dorado."

"And into the present day. Two months ago, an Ethiopian prince offered to purchase the Valiant gold."

His family's treasure was more than a showpiece; it was collateral. If Marian was right and the company was on the brink of disaster, they could sell the gold—a worst-case scenario.

She tapped the glass wall. "This doesn't seem like enough protection."

"The glass is reinforced and the steel bars are unbreakable. The only way to open these doors is with a code and two simultaneous fingerprints from Spencer heirs. That includes me, my brother, Uncle Samuel and a cousin who's currently on an expedition to the North Pole."

"What about your mother?"

"Mom passed away when I was just a kid."

"I'm sorry.... Do I see a safe in the corner behind the gold?"

He nodded. "There's family jewelry in there. Ironically, the diamonds are probably worth as much as the gold. It's too bad those necklaces and rings are almost never worn."

"A real shame." She pivoted and looked up at him. "Diamonds are meant to be seen."

He would have liked nothing more than to retrieve one of the ornate necklaces from the safe, drape it around her throat and make love to her on the Valiant gold. "I wish I could show you."

"There's something magical about precious gems. I got to wear a very valuable rented bracelet once." She gestured gracefully. "Rubies and diamonds."

"You must have been attending an important event."

"The Governor's Inaugural Ball. He's a friend of my ex."

Nick was getting curious about the ex's identity. "I'm surprised I didn't see you there."

"I've always been good at fading into the wallpaper, even when I'm wearing diamonds."

"You look plenty sparkling to me."

He heard a loud pop. A gunshot?

Grabbing Kelly's wrist, he pulled her out of the vault and shut the door. As he ran toward the exit from the conference room, he shouted to her, "Stay back."

In the hallway, Marian poked her head out of her office and called to him. "The noise sounded like it came from your uncle's office."

"Was it a gun?"

"I think so."

A moment ago, he'd thought the worst fate that could befall the Spencers was to lose the gold. He hadn't considered physical harm to his family. At the door to his uncle's office, Nick grasped the handle. It was locked. "Samuel, open up. Samuel? Are you all right?"

There was no reply. If there was a gunman in the office, Nick should proceed carefully. But if Samuel had been shot, they had to get in there and help him.

Marian grasped his sleeve. "Don't you have a key in your office?"

"That's all the way upstairs. It'll take too long."

In a few strides, he was at the glass display case beside the prospector painting. Fortunately, the case wasn't locked. Nick reached inside and wrapped his fingers around a pickax from the 1800s.

At the door to his uncle's office, he used the tool to break the latch before he kicked the door open. The smell of gunpowder hung in the air. There was no one in the room except for his white-haired Uncle Samuel who sprawled on the floor beside his desk. Blood spread in a dark stain on the beige carpet. A .45 caliber gun was in his right hand.

Nick knelt beside the old man and felt for a pulse. "He's still breathing. Call 911."

Kelly joined him on the floor. "Let me take care of him. I'm a nurse."

"You deliver babies."

"I'm also an RN. Step back, Nick."

He gently removed the gun from his uncle's limp hand and stood, looking down as Kelly tried to stop the bleeding from a chest wound.

The door had been locked. The windows were closed.

A set of blueprints lay on the desk. Across them, his uncle had written two words: *I'm Sorry.*

# Chapter Three

*Monday, 10:25 a.m.*

"It's not your fault that he died."

"I know," Kelly said.

Her friend Serena Bellows motioned for her to come out from behind the kitchen counter and join her in the living room. Picking her way through a minefield of toys and stuffed animals, Kelly made her way across the large room with the cathedral-style ceiling. Over the years, Serena and Nigel's farmhouse on a twenty-acre spread had grown from a small cabin to a sprawling four-bedroom house.

Serena liked to say that the house had grown

organically. The original cabin was long, flat and ranch-style. The living room and attached kitchen fit into an A-frame with solar panels on the roof. A Victorian tower housed Nigel's home office. There were no predominant colors. Instead, the walls varied from room to room in a veritable rainbow.

"Sit," Serena said. "Talk to me."

Coffee mug in hand, Kelly sank onto the sofa. "I already told you what happened last night."

"But you haven't told me the whole story, and you need to let it out." Holding her six-day-old daughter, Serena occupied a large oak rocking chair by the fireplace. She unbuttoned her turquoise muslin blouse and prepared to start breast-feeding. "I can feel your grief."

Kelly couldn't deny her sadness. Though she'd never met Nick's uncle while he was alive, she would forever be connected to Samuel Spencer. For a few moments, she'd held his life in her hands. "I wish I could have done more for him."

She'd worked hard to keep his heart beating

and to stanch the bleeding from the gunshot wound. The paramedics had arrived eighteen minutes after Nick called 911. At that time, Samuel still had a pulse. Nick had gone with the ambulance while she and Marian had stayed behind to talk with the police. Less than an hour later, she'd learned that Samuel never regained consciousness and had died on the operating table. Logically, she knew that Serena was right and Samuel's death wasn't her fault, but it always hurt to lose a patient.

"Have you ever wondered," Serena asked, "why people like you and me choose to be midwives and not surgeons?"

"Because medical school is really expensive?"

"As midwives, we get to help people. Most important, there's almost always a happy ending."

Kelly knew exactly what she was talking about. Unlike the nurses who worked in emergency rooms and faced life-and-death situations every day, midwives brought new life into the world. It was a great job. She loved hearing the first cries of a newborn, feeling the grip of a tiny hand around her finger and seeing a perfect cherub face.

Smiling, she watched her friend breast-feed her infant. For the first time this morning, she felt something resembling calm. Serena's husband had taken the other three kids and Serena's sister to the grocery store. Though Kelly enjoyed staying with the raucous family with the totally appropriate last name of Bellows, she needed her moments of silence. Leaning back against the yellow-and-green-patterned sofa cushions, she sipped her coffee and said, "This is nice."

"Being around all these kids and animals drives you crazy, doesn't it?"

"It's different." She had only one younger sister who had stayed in the Chicago area near their parents. "I've never been part of a big family."

"You are now," Serena said. "You're one of us, and you'll never be alone again."

"Is that a threat?"

"It's a promise. If you ever need a friend, I've got your back."

"That goes both ways," Kelly said.

She and Serena had been buddies since freshman year at the University of Colorado in Boulder. Even though they'd lived apart, they were as close as two friends could be. But they weren't family, not really. Kelly had always wanted children of her own.

Serena adjusted the baby at her breast. "Are you ready to talk about last night?"

She inhaled a deep breath and started talking. "My first reaction was panic. A ringing in my ears. Inability to breathe. Momentary paralysis. It was scary. We had to use a pickax to break the door down."

"Then the adrenaline kicked in."

She nodded. When she saw the wounded man, Kelly knew what needed to be done. Her mind was clear, and her hands were steady. She remembered procedures she hadn't used in years. "It was only after the paramedics took him away that I became aware of what had happened. I had blood all over my clothes. The scarf you gave me was destroyed."

"The Kelly-green scarf?"

"It's so corny that you got me a Kelly-green scarf."

"What happened to it?"

"I used it to stanch the blood flow." The memory caused her hand to shake, and she set down the coffee mug. "That poor man committed suicide."

"Are you sure about that? Most suicides don't shoot themselves in the gut."

"That was what the police said. They kept asking me if I saw powder burns on his shirt." She'd torn away his clothing to get to the wound. "I couldn't tell. There was too much blood."

"Did the police think it was suicide?"

"There will be an investigation, for sure.

But he was in a locked room with the murder weapon in his hand, and he'd left a note that said he was sorry."

"How did you find out that he'd died?" Serena asked.

"Nick called."

"Nick Spencer?"

Kelly nodded. "He called me on his cell phone from the hospital. The doctors had gotten his uncle into the operating room when his heart stopped. They couldn't revive him."

She didn't know Nick well, but she'd recognized the pain in his voice. His words were flat and hollow as though he was speaking from the bottom of a deep well.

"What else did he say?" Serena asked.

"The paramedics told him that I did a good job. He thanked me for trying to save his uncle."

Last night, she'd wanted to comfort him, and she was a little disappointed that he hadn't called her this morning. Not that she had any right to expect him to contact her; she barely knew the man. Dealing with his uncle's suicide, Nick probably had his hands full.

"Nick Spencer," Serena said. "He's big and tall, am I right? And good-looking?"

"Last night, he was wearing a tux."

"Yum." Serena tucked her breast back into her nursing bra. Cradling her infant, she gently rocked. "I think you should call him to offer condolences. Better yet, you should stop by his place and take him a homemade pie."

"Why would I do that?"

"Well, he just might need a shoulder to cry on. Or a hand to hold. You know, human warmth."

"Are you suggesting that I take advantage of a tragic situation to make a move on Nick?"

"I'm just saying that you're both single and there must have been a reason you were alone with him on the ninth floor of the Spencer Building."

"He showed me the gold."

"Wow! Nigel is going to be so jealous. He does work for a client in that building, and he's

never seen the gold. Nick must really like you."
Serena was on a roll, talking fast. "This is excellent, really excellent. If you and Nick hit it off, you'll be motivated to stay in Valiant, and I'll have a partner. This is so, so, so perfect."

Kelly chuckled. "So this is about giving me a reason to stay and be your partner. It's all about you."

"I'm thinking of you," she said with a grin. "Honey, you could do a lot worse than Nick Spencer."

Kelly couldn't argue that point. Nick was handsome, sexy, funny, capable and rich. "If he's such a catch, how come some other woman hasn't snapped him up?"

"He's only been divorced for a couple of years. From what I hear, he's a devoted daddy."

She didn't know he had children. "How many kids?"

"Two daughters, I think they're seven and four. Beautiful girls, I've seen them in Valiant with Nick but I think they live in Denver with their mom. Both girls have black hair and blue eyes like their father."

The front doorbell chimed, and Kelly rose from the sofa. "Don't move. I'll get it."

She rushed to the front door. The first ringing of the chimes hadn't wakened the baby, and she wanted to make sure there wouldn't be a second bell. She whipped open the door and looked out through the screen.

Standing on the covered porch was a man in a black suit. Though he couldn't have been more than forty, his close-cropped hair was completely white. With his square jaw and angry eyes, he would have been intimidating if he hadn't been standing beside a white goat with a black face and black splotches like polka dots decorating her round belly.

The goat, whose name was Fifi, tapped her hooves on the porch, rubbed against his trouser leg and bleated. She liked being around people, especially men.

Stifling a chuckle, Kelly asked, "May I help you?"

"Are you Kelly Evans?"

"Yes."

"I'd like to ask you a couple of questions about last night." He reached inside his jacket pocket, took out a gold card case, peeled one off and held it toward her. "Y. E. Trask, private investigator."

As she opened the screen door to take his card, Kelly decided that she didn't want to invite him into the house. Grabbing her denim jacket from a peg by the door, she stepped outside. There was something about this man that she didn't trust, and she wanted to keep him away from Serena's family.

"There isn't much to say, Mr. Trask. I already gave my statement to the police."

"I wanted to hear your story. In your own words." Fifi butted his thigh, and he lurched forward. The goat bleated. Trask cursed. "Aren't these animals supposed to be in a pen?"

"Well, yes, but they're good at escaping. If you pay some attention to her, she might leave you alone."

"I've found the opposite to be true," he said curtly. "If I pay attention to a female, she tends to stick around, even when she's not wanted."

This was a guy she definitely didn't want to spend time with. "Fifi isn't like that."

"Don't waste my time, Ms. Evans. Are you going to help me or not? The family has concerns."

If he'd told her right away that he worked for the Spencers, she would have been more cooperative. Looking down the driveway, she spotted the family van approaching the house. In a few moments, Nigel and the kids would be back and they'd be surrounded by chaos. "Come with me. We'll find somewhere quiet to talk."

Waving to the van, she directed Trask across the farmyard toward the barn. Two spotted goats trotted side by side as though they had an important mission. One of the llamas strolled past the chicken coops, creating a flurry of angry hens.

Most people would have been amused. Not only was there a varied and interesting menagerie, but the lower two feet of the barn was painted with wild artwork by the kids. It was kind of adorable, but Trask was all business. His primary concern seemed to be to avoid stepping on anything ugly and messing up his wingtip shoes.

By the corral fence, she found a space. "Ask your questions."

"You were the first person to touch Samuel after entering the room," he said. "Is that correct?"

"Actually, Nick was the first. He found a pulse, and then I stepped in."

"Assuming that Samuel committed suicide, can you speculate on how he did it?"

"He must have been standing because his body was beside the desk rather than behind it. He still had the gun in his hand. I'd guess that he turned the weapon toward himself and pulled the trigger."

"He was still alive when you started treating him. Did he speak?"

"He was mumbling, but he wasn't conscious." The police had asked her about this several times, and she knew that a dying declaration would be important. "I've been trying to remember if he said anything coherent, but none of it made sense. First he said to close the door. He repeated the word 'gold' several times. And he talked about a heart of stone."

When Fifi came toward them, Trask glared. His expression was so angry that Kelly thought he might pull a gun and shoot the cheerful goat. Fifi turned tail and bounded away.

"Is there anything else, Mr. Trask?"

"Concentrate, Ms. Evans. What did he say about the heart of stone?"

"It didn't make sense." She thought for a moment then shook her head. "Sorry. I'm not even sure if those were his words."

"I don't like surprises," he said. "If you're holding back, we're going to have a problem."

Was he threatening her? "Why would I hold anything back?"

He didn't answer. Instead, he focused his angry glare at her. She stared right back at him. Kelly wasn't a silly goat like Fifi, and she refused to be intimidated.

She snapped, "Are we done?"

"I'll be in touch."

He pivoted and strode away from her. She imagined that being a private investigator wasn't a pleasant job; you'd be spying on people, confronting them and serving them with legal papers. Y. E. Trask seemed to have exactly the right temperament for his work—hostile, aggressive and a little nasty.

It bothered her that Nick had sent Trask to interview her without letting her know. He should have warned her that a creepy white-haired man would show up on Serena's doorstep and accuse her of holding back. Something about this wasn't right. She decided to talk to Nick.

Her cell phone was in the pocket of the denim jacket she'd grabbed before coming outside. She pulled it out and redialed the number he'd used last night to call her from the hospital. When he answered, she almost hung up. What had she been thinking? Nick had just lost a close family member; she shouldn't be bothering him because a private eye was rude to her.

"How are you doing?" she asked.

"Been better," he said. "I've been thinking about you. I wanted to thank you again for the way you jumped in and tried to save my uncle."

"I'm glad to help in any way I can. I tried to answer questions for your private investigator, but I think I made him angry."

"What are you talking about?"

"The guy you sent out to Serena's house. He's an investigator working for your family. His name is Y. E. Trask. He has white hair."

"Hold on." She could hear him talking to

someone else but couldn't tell what he was saying until he came back on the line. "Kelly, nobody has ever heard of him. He doesn't work
for us."

Who sent him? And why?

# Chapter Four

During the drive from Valiant to Serena's farm, Nick was steamed. He hated that Kelly was being harassed. She was completely innocent— a bystander who happened to be in the wrong place at the wrong time.

When he got her phone call, he'd been tangled in a mass of corporate red tape generated by the lawyers, the police, his family and employees. Everyone looked to him—as the most senior member of the Spencer clan—to make the necessary decisions. Nick was expected to step up and take control.

Truth be told, he was probably the least informed person in the room. Working out of his office in Breckenridge, he managed to avoid most of the corporate decisions. That was his brother's job. Unfortunately, Jared was still in Singapore.

At a mailbox painted with flowers and butterflies, he made a left turn and drove down a long, curving driveway. Hearing Kelly's voice had given him a focus—a problem he could deal with. He needed to find out who had contacted her and why and, most of all, if she was in any kind of danger from this fake investigator.

Though he'd never been to the farm owned by Serena and Nigel Bellows, he knew he was in the right place when he saw the farmhouse—a mash-up of architectural styles that Marian had described as crazy. From modern A-frame to the Victorian tower topped by an ornate weather vane to the wild splashes of color painted on the barn, none of the construction made sense. And yet, he felt a genuine smile tug at the corners of his mouth as he parked and got out of his SUV.

In keeping with the fanciful atmosphere, a fat goat sashayed toward him, followed by a little blond girl wearing a yellow sweatshirt and a tiara. "You will be the prince," she said to him. "You're supposed to slay the dragon. It's your job."

He reached down and scratched the goat between her floppy ears. "Is this the dragon?"

"That's a goat, silly. It's Fifi."

"And what's your name?"

She flipped her hair away from her small, freckled face. "I'm Princess Butterfly."

She was a ray of sunshine on a cloudy day. He wanted to hug Princess Butterfly and her pet goat for reminding him that being irritated by lawyers and accountants was a sheer waste of time. If he wanted to get the job done, he had to step up and slay the corporate dragon.

Kelly raced around the corner of the house, wearing a red sheet as a cape and a cardboard hat with scales and spikes. Her brown sweat-shirt was raggedy and oversized. Two other small children and a llama accompanied her.

"Hi, Nick." She gave him a little wave, and then she roared. "The dragon is nigh."

Princess Butterfly ducked behind him. "Get her."

He braced himself and pointed imperiously toward Kelly. "No way, dragon. I banish you."

She whipped off her cape and hat as she collapsed into the dirt. "Oh, no, I'm melting."

All the kids ran to help her. "No, dragon, don't die. That's not how it works."

She stopped melting. "It's not?"

"No," they chorused. "You turn into another princess."

"Okay." She popped back up. "I'm Princess Kelly."

After a few more reassurances, she sent the children back to the house and came toward him. Her straight hair was messy from being a half-melted dragon, and she tucked the loose strands behind her ears. "Thanks for playing along."

"I didn't know you were so ferocious."

"Oh, yeah, I'm a fire-breather." She picked up the sheet and folded it under her arm. "You really didn't need to come all the way out here. I could have driven into town."

"Seeing this house is worth the drive."

"Unusual, huh?"

"I've never experienced anything like it." And that was saying a lot. Nick had a master's degree in architecture and had designed hotels, condos and custom houses. "I did a house in Aspen that looks like a flying saucer, and a Gothic-type castle for a rock star. Fun projects, but not as unique as this farmhouse."

"The people who live here make it happy and interesting."

"That's always true. A house is only a shell."

She reached toward him and lightly rested her hand on his sleeve. Her chin tilted up, and her pale green eyes scanned his face as though searching for something important. "I'm sorry about your uncle's death."

Other people had offered condolences, but he sensed true empathy from her. "I appreciate your concern."

"Tell me about Samuel."

"He was a crazy old man, eccentric as hell." That was the standard line. Most people would describe his uncle that way, but Nick appreciated the creativity that came along with Samuel's unusual perspective. "I admired his talent. We didn't talk every day or even every month. But we were close. Maybe it was the DNA, but I understood who he was. At least, I thought I did."

Without another word, she wrapped her arms around his waist and rested her head on his chest. Her touch reached through the wall of self-control he'd built to keep going. There wasn't time to fall apart; he needed to take care of business.

Nick hadn't cried for his uncle, hadn't shed

a tear or acknowledged the pain of losing him, but as he enfolded her in his embrace, raw emotion poured through his veins. His sadness was tempered by anger. How could Samuel commit suicide? Why would he choose death? Nick should have been more aware of his uncle's state of mind, should have talked to him, should have seen his desperation.

He lowered his head and rubbed his cheek against her silky hair while inhaling the strawberry scent of her shampoo. Holding Kelly grounded him and gave him clarity. "I'm going to miss him."

"He was a part of your life."

She shifted her weight and leaned back. Just as easily as they had come together, they separated. It surprised him that he didn't feel uncomfortable about their embrace. Having Kelly in his arms felt like the most natural thing in the world.

"I'm glad I came out here," he said. "I like

seeing you, and I needed a break from Marian and the lawyers."

"Did any of them know Trask?"

"No." Time to get down to business. "Show me his card."

She dug into the pocket of her jeans and pulled out a plain, white card with the name, occupation and a phone number. "He seemed real concerned about Samuel's dying words, and he didn't believe me when I said I didn't remember him saying anything that made sense."

Nick recalled the scene from last night. When Kelly took over with his uncle, he had stepped aside. "I wasn't aware that he said anything."

"He was barely conscious, mumbling. He told me to close the door. I guess he was talking about the door we crashed through."

There was one other door in the room, the door to a closet. Though he'd assumed that Samuel committed suicide, Nick had opened that door and looked inside to make sure no one was hiding there. "What else?"

"Gold," she said. "He repeated it several times. And he said something about a heart of stone or a stone heart. It reminded me of a lyric in a country-western song. Does it mean anything to you?"

He shook his head. "You said that Trask didn't believe you. What made you think that?"

Her lips pulled into a frown. "He told me that I'd better not be holding anything back."

"That sounds like a threat."

"I'm not sure if it was meant that way." Her frown deepened. "Trask is a very unpleasant person."

"I don't like him snooping around," Nick said.

"Neither do I, especially since he came here. If Trask is dangerous, I don't want him near Serena and the children."

"Agreed," he said. "We'll get to the bottom of this as soon as possible. Would you mind coming back to the Spencer Building with me?"

"Not a problem. But I'll need to change into a more presentable jacket."

"I like the threadbare dragon look." He fell into step beside her as they approached the house. "How many people live here?"

"Serena and Nigel have three children and an infant. Serena's sister is also staying here for a couple of weeks to help out. I'm sharing a bedroom with her."

"How long are you planning to stay in the area?"

"I'm not sure." She gave a little shrug. "When Serena called and asked me to help with her clients while she was taking care of her baby, I realized how much I missed Colorado. I've always loved the mountains, and this feels like home to me. I gave up my apartment in Austin."

"That sounds like a permanent move." And he was glad to hear it. He wanted to get to know Kelly better, which might take more than a couple of weeks. "Are you planning to stay here with Serena?"

"God, no. I love her and adore her kids, but I'd go mad if I lived here. I need my privacy."

When she pushed open the door to an open room with cathedral ceilings, they walked into a recital of something that sounded like "Twinkle, Twinkle, Little Star." All three kids were singing and banging on various types of drums while their parents watched and dutifully applauded before welcoming Nick into their home.

Nick shook hands with Nigel, who looked familiar. "Have you done work at the Spencer Building?"

"Private contracting with a couple of the software firms," he said. "My wife tells me that you showed Kelly the gold."

*Everybody loved that gold.* "If you'd like to see it, let me know when you're coming by."

"You bet I will."

Serena, with her beautiful baby in her arms, joined them. She allowed him one peek at the infant who was, miraculously, sleeping. Then she got right to the point. "You and Kelly have made a connection. I couldn't be happier."

"A connection?"

"She's ready to settle down," Serena said, "and I want her to stay in Valiant and help me build my business."

Kelly popped up beside him. Still wearing her khaki pants, she'd changed into a lightweight burgundy jacket. "We have to go."

"Stay," Serena cajoled. "There's so much more I have to tell Nick about you."

Teasing, Nick said, "And I want to hear it all."

"Not today." She linked her arm with his and pulled him toward the door. "Serena, I have my cell if you need me."

On the porch, she exhaled in a whoosh. "I bet you didn't know you'd volunteered to be on the Serena Bellows version of the dating game."

"I like her and Nigel." Fifi trotted by carrying the red dragon cape in her mouth. "And the whole menagerie."

With all this rampant energy and enthusiasm, he'd forgotten that he'd come here to make sure Kelly wasn't being harassed or threatened by Trask. As they walked toward his SUV, he was reminded of the possible danger. Parked at the end of the winding drive that led to the Bellowses' house was a black stretch limousine.

Kelly saw it, too. "Do you know who that is?"

"I intend to find out." He paused outside the driver's-side door to his SUV. "You should go back to the house while I talk to them."

"If this has something to do with Samuel's death and his last words, the people in the limo might be looking for me," she said. "I'm coming with you."

He didn't argue. "I'll drive. I want the limo to follow us. If it stays here, Princess Butterfly and the goats might decide to check it out."

"That can't happen." Her voice was determined. "If anybody scares these kids, I'll have to kill them."

"You bloodthirsty dragons are all alike."

He brought her around to the passenger side and opened the door for her. Though Nick was keeping the tone light so Kelly wouldn't be worried, he had misgivings. Why was a limo here? What the hell were they after?

He drove down the driveway toward the cheerful mailbox and made a right turn as though heading back to Valiant. As he'd expected, the limo followed on the two-lane asphalt road. The way he saw it, there were two options: contact the police or face the limo himself.

Thus far, he hadn't been impressed with the local cops or the Colorado Bureau of Investigation agents. They'd been quick to accept that Samuel committed suicide, and the case was closed. Nick thought there was a lot more to be investigated, and he was going to have to be more involved.

Kelly had her cell phone in hand. "Should I call 911?"

"Not yet. I want to see what they're up to."

The SUV was approaching the unmanned volunteer fire department building, a good place to pull over. Nick signaled a turn and stepped on the brake.

"Do you have a gun?" she asked.

He was an architect, not a sharpshooter. "I'm just going to talk to them. You stay in the car and lock the doors. Get behind the steering wheel so we can make a fast getaway if we need to."

"I really don't like the way that sounds."

"This isn't going to be a problem. I'll be back here before you know it."

He opened his car door and got out. At the same time, the limo driver emerged. A stocky guy with a thick neck, he looked as if he could also be a bodyguard.

"Mr. Spencer," he said, "Mr. Radcliff will see you now."

His civilized attitude didn't fit with the situation. "Why were you following me?"

"Convenience."

He held open the rear door to the limo, and Nick entered. He hoped he'd be able to come back out in one piece.

# Chapter Five

In the rearview mirror, Kelly watched Nick disappear into the back of the long stretch limousine with tinted windows. It worried her that she couldn't see him. She held up her cell phone, ready to call the police at the slightest sign of trouble.

The limo driver closed the door behind Nick and strolled around the car toward the gleaming front grill where he leaned against the fender and gazed across the road into the forested area on the other side. Though his attitude was relaxed, he looked like the kind of guy who would carry a gun and know how to use it. Why was she thinking about guns? Maybe she'd been in Texas too long.

She checked the mirror again. Sunlight flashed off the silver chrome. She hated limos. Her ex had always insisted on taking a limo when they went to gala events because he liked to make an entrance. In his tailored tuxedo with his diamond-stud cuff links, Ted Maxwell was a very handsome man. Heads always turned when he walked by.

And she had followed in his wake, aware that she'd never be as pretty as he was. He'd tried to coach her about what to wear and how to behave. The only bit of grooming that had really worked was the way she'd highlighted her straight brown hair, which was the only thing she'd kept after the divorce. According to Ted, he'd fought to become an associate partner at a top Denver law firm before he was thirty-five. He'd done the hard work, and all she had to do—her only real job as his wife—was to look good and back him up. She'd been a miserable failure, emphasis on the *miserable*.

Not only had she been a dud when it came to style, but her profession hadn't been classy enough for his society friends. When he introduced her, he'd always said she was in medicine, rather than admitting that she was only a nurse.

That snub had been the final straw. She'd always been proud of what she did and refused to pretend otherwise. Instead of trailing behind him in uncomfortable and ridiculously expensive high heels, she'd opted out of the fancy dress balls and political fundraisers. Better to stay home with a good book.

His new wife must be more adept at gorgeousness. Kelly had heard that they were a power couple on their way into the national political arena. They already had one child, even though Ted hadn't been interested in children when he was with her.

She checked the mirror again, hoping to see Nick coming toward her. No such luck. It was kind of a bad omen that when she met him, he was wearing a tux. Was he anything like her ex? Ted had more polish, but Nick was definitely a head-turner. Handsome and rich made for a dangerous combination. Even though Nick seemed funny and down-to-earth and had complimented her on her nursing skills, she'd keep her eyes wide-open. The first time he insisted that she slip into a pair of four-inch heels, she was out of there.

Nervous, she turned around in the seat to stare at the car behind her. Oh, yeah, she hated limos.

THE PLUSH, BEIGE LEATHER interior of the limo reminded Nick less of luxury and more of a mobile office. The pudgy, little man who introduced himself as Barry Radcliff sat on the bench seat at the rear behind a narrow desk that swung out from the wall. A laptop was open in front of him. A computer printer and fax were on a shelf below the partition separating them from the driver.

The most interesting piece of equipment was a leggy brunette with a short skirt and gladiator sandals. Her loose, curly hair tumbled past the deep vee in her cream-colored silk blouse. Barry introduced her as his attorney.

"And don't let her beauty fool you," Radcliff said. "Francine graduated from Stanford Law School cum laude and almost qualified for the Olympics."

"What sport?" Nick asked.

"Beach volleyball."

"Of course." This day was getting more and more bizarre. Nick sprawled back in the seat on the left side of the limo, surprised that there was enough room for his long legs. "Why do you want to see me?"

"Your uncle, God rest his soul, did some business with me. I want to make sure it's taken care of."

"I'm the wrong person to contact. You should be dealing with the attorney at Spencer Enterprises."

"That's not my style."

Radcliff's style was questionable. He wore a loose-fitting blue-and-gold-striped shirt with the top four buttons unfastened to show off his heavy gold necklaces. His dark hair was thick and combed straight back. He had the kind of tan that went with spending a lot of time on a boat or a golf course.

"Your uncle," Radcliff said, "borrowed a million dollars from me. Payback was due on the day he died. I want my money."

"You'll have to be patient. My uncle had a substantial estate, but there are probate concerns."

"Which is why I'm coming to you, Nick. I'll give you until next week to make good on the loan. After Tuesday of next week, I'll be taking my payment in collateral."

Inwardly, Nick groaned. "Let me guess. My uncle used the Valiant gold as collateral."

"Bingo." He leaned back in his seat. "Show him the agreement, honey."

Apparently, the Stanford-trained, volleyball-playing attorney didn't mind being called honey. She reached into a file folder and produced a copy of a one-page document, which she held toward Nick.

He skimmed it quickly. Two months ago, just after the first of the year, Samuel had borrowed one million cash. If the amount, plus a couple hundred thousand in interest, was not paid within one week from when it was due, Radcliff was entitled to the equivalent amount in Valiant gold. The signature on the bottom was Samuel's.

"It looks pretty straightforward," Nick said. "But I still need to have the legal department check it out."

"This isn't a corporate issue. The loan was man to man, between me and Samuel, God rest his soul. That's why I came to you as a member of the Spencer family."

"Do you have any idea why he needed the money?"

"Not my concern." Radcliff waved his pudgy hand in front of his face. He was beginning to sound agitated. "Can I count on you or not?"

"Let me think."

Nick would have been justified in pitching the document out the window and letting Radcliff's sexy attorney drag this debt through the courts for settlement. But he felt an obligation to his uncle to honor this debt. Samuel had thought this money was important enough to gamble the family treasure. Finding the project he was working on might help Nick understand why his uncle had committed suicide.

"I have a question for you," Nick said. "Did Samuel seem depressed to you? Or nervous? Scared?"

"He was okay. I liked the old guy. He was a risk taker, you know what I mean? These days, decisions get made by committees and everybody is busy covering their butt. Samuel had guts, God rest his soul."

That wasn't the description of a man who

was about to kill himself. As far as Nick was concerned, Radcliff had a better idea of Samuel than half the people who claimed to know him well. In his way, Radcliff was an honorable man.

"I'll get the money."

"Too bad," Radcliff said. "I had my heart set on that gold."

Nick reached for the door handle. "Next time you want to reach me, use the phone."

"When I meet a person for the first time, I want to look him in the eye."

Not a bad policy. Nick was beginning to like this guy. "How do I contact you?"

Radcliff nodded to his lawyer, and she leaned forward to hand him a card. The view down her blouse was a major distraction. If this settlement ever got to court, he'd bet on her to win.

Exiting the limo, he nodded to the driver, went to the passenger side of his SUV and climbed in. When he closed the door, he looked down at the copy of the document in his hand. Radcliff's business card had listings for five different companies—three of them appeared to be associated with oil drilling.

"What happened?" Kelly asked. "Are you okay?"

"Confused as hell," he admitted. "The inside of that limo is like an office on wheels, and the guy behind the desk is Barry Radcliff. He's one of those guys with a dark tan and gold jewelry, maybe from Miami or Vegas. Or maybe he just plays a lot of golf, I don't know."

"You're rambling, Nick."

"Radcliff loaned my uncle a million dollars."

"Whoa." She sat back behind the steering wheel. "That's a big loan."

He agreed. Coming up with a million in cash wouldn't be easy. As Marian Whitman kept telling him, Spencer Enterprises was stretched to the max. Last night when she wanted him to confront his uncle, she intended to close down some of the projects he'd been developing. Big mistake. Samuel didn't know the meaning of "no." He'd gone elsewhere for financing.

The limo pulled even with his SUV, and the rear window partially rolled down. A slender, feminine hand reached out and waved goodbye before the traveling office drove away.

"Who's the woman?" Kelly asked.

"Radcliff's attorney. She's an Olympic-caliber athlete in beach volleyball."

"Sure she is. And I'm a supermodel."

"I know this sounds crazy," he said, "but this is a copy of a legitimate document, signed by my uncle. He used the Valiant gold as collateral."

"Settling debts sounds like a job for Marian Whitman. She's in charge of the money, right? Why did Radcliff contact you?"

"Because he's a smart guy. He knows I'm more likely to pay him back than Marian or any other corporate officer."

For Nick, the debt wasn't about the money. He was motivated by concern for his uncle. More than anything else, he needed to find out what had caused Samuel to take his own life and scribble a note that said he was sorry. Apologizing was out of character. His uncle was the kind of man—the gutsy kind of man—who faced his mistakes and made them right.

Kelly rested her hands on the steering wheel. "Where do we go from here?"

"I've got to find out why Samuel needed a million dollars and what he was working on."

"There must be records or blueprints or something," she said. "Can we check his computer?"

"He barely kept track of what he was doing, hated using the computer." But Nick knew how to get the information they needed. "Change seats with me. We're going to see Julia."

He exited the passenger side and came around the SUV. The conversation with Radcliff had given him new energy and strength. Instead of dull gray sadness, he had hope for finding out what happened. In the driver's seat, he started the engine.

"Who's Julia?" Kelly asked.

"Julia Starkey has been my uncle's secretary for as long as I can remember. She came to work for him, probably thirty years ago, as a single mom with two young kids. They fell in love."

"You're going to have to fill in the blanks," Kelly said. "Did Samuel have a wife when he fell in love with his secretary?"

"He never married. As far as I know, Julia was the only woman in his life. You'll understand what I mean when you see her house. It's an expression of his feelings for her."

"Like the Taj Mahal."

"That's a tomb," he said. "Julia's house was designed for a living woman who appreciates the serenity of orderly surroundings. There's something mysterious about the place. Uncle Samuel used to say that no matter how much time he spent with Julia, he'd never completely understand her."

When he was a teenager, Nick had helped his

uncle build Julia's house, and his opinion of the property was colored by that experience. During that summer, he'd learned a lot about architecture. The mathematics and calculations of creating blueprints were only part of design. Samuel taught him about heart, about making a house into a home.

At a road leading into a mountain canyon, he took a right turn. Earlier today when he was at the Spencer Building, he'd noticed that Julia's office, which was right next door to his uncle's, was empty. Nobody expected her to come to work. Samuel's death had to be harder on her than anyone else.

He looked over at Kelly. "You're quiet."

"I was trying to imagine what it would be like to have someone love you so much that they built you a house." She gave him a wistful smile. "It's epic."

He wanted to tell her that every woman deserved a castle and a man who loved her so deeply that he would shape his life around her wants and needs, but he wasn't that much of a romantic. Real life was seldom that pretty. "Don't get the wrong idea. Julia and Samuel weren't a lovey-dovey couple. He was a dreamer, and she was pragmatic. They argued all the time."

"And he never married her." Her eyebrows pulled down into a frown. "I guess no relationship is perfect."

Perfection was too much to hope for. He'd gladly settle for what Samuel had with Julia.

# Chapter Six

*Monday, 2:25 p.m.*

After Nick's description, Kelly expected a gigantic mansion or, at least, a couple of turrets. Instead, she saw a home built of dark wood and lots of windows, many of which were stained glass that sparkled like exotic jewels in the forested surroundings. Rather than reaching for the sky, Julia's house was primarily horizontal, gradually rising to three stories. If they hadn't taken a turn at the driveway, she might have driven right by the place.

"It's kind of secretive," she said.

"So is Julia."

The afternoon sunlight shone brightly on the large wooden deck nearest the driveway. Under the eaves, Kelly noticed the figure of a tall, thin woman who stood in the shadows with her arms folded across her middle. She didn't look welcoming. "Maybe we should have called before dropping by."

"Julia is practically my aunt," he said. "Besides, she might have told me not to come, and I need to find out about Samuel's latest project."

He parked in front of a three-car garage, and they climbed a winding path that led to the front entryway. As they approached, the details of the house became clear. Surrounding the path and all along the side of the house, Samuel had used xeriscaping techniques that wouldn't require watering, which was always a problem in the arid Colorado climate. The placement of rocks and plants reminded her of a Japanese garden, and she heard the gentle echo of a wind chime. There didn't seem to be a right angle anywhere. Some of the wood beams featured delicate carv-

ings or calligraphy. The most interesting feature was the play of light through blue, purple,
red and green stained-glass pieces that created
an ever-changing mosaic of color.

If this house truly represented the woman who
lived here, Kelly expected to find someone of
hidden depth and passion.

When Julia answered the bell, Kelly was a
little disappointed. The tall, thin woman was
dressed in a shapeless brown skirt and a top in
a similar dull color. Her faded gray hair was
cut short to frame her angular face. She didn't
seem remarkable at all.

Nick introduced her, and Kelly shook Julia's
cold hand. "I'm sorry for you loss," she said.

"You're the nurse who was with Samuel when
he died."

"Before he died," Kelly corrected. "He was
barely conscious."

"Could he speak?"

"A little bit." Like everyone else, she wanted
to hear Samuel's last words.

"Did he say my name?"

Kelly's heart went out to this sad-looking woman in her beautiful but empty house. Julia wanted to know if she was in her lover's thoughts when he knew he was dying. "I'm sorry."

"That's typical. He always took me for granted." She opened the door wider. "Would you like to come in?"

Nick strode into the gracious flagstone foyer as though he belonged there. "I'm hoping you can help me. I have some questions about Samuel's death."

"His suicide," she said. "Isn't that what the police are saying? He committed suicide?"

"That seems to be the expert opinion. The security cameras outside the elevators didn't show anyone leaving. The one on the tenth floor was out, but that shouldn't make a difference because Samuel's office was on nine. His office door was locked, and the gun was in his hand."

"I know about the gun." She led them into a

sunken living room with a massive stone fire-place. Only a few paintings were hung, but the light from the stained glass decorated the walls. "The police spoke to me. They wanted to know if Samuel usually kept his .45 at the office."

"Did he?"

"He carried his gun in the glove compartment when he was on the road, and he's been travel-ing a lot. I assume he didn't want to leave it in his car."

"Where has he been going?"

"Hell if I know. He never tells me anything anymore." Her tone was harsh, angry. "Can I offer you a cup of tea?"

"That would be great," Nick said. "Do you mind if I show Kelly your house?"

"I'd rather you didn't go into the bedroom. Otherwise, feel free to look around. This place is a tribute to your uncle. As long as I live here, you're welcome to come and visit."

Nick led the way from the large living room and down a hallway to a combination study and sitting room. All the while, he pointed out the features. "There's no wasted space. Even the hallway has an area for sitting, and windows looking out on a fountain and a stone Buddha. Transition from one room to another is a pleasure."

His enthusiasm was as endearing as his love for his uncle. Nick appreciated architecture. Like her, he loved his work. But she had the distinct impression that he wasn't fond of the corporate responsibilities that came with being a Spencer heir.

"There's a secret passageway in the house," he confided. "I can't show it to you because it's in the bedroom, but it's pretty cool. If you didn't know it was there, you'd never find it."

"Why put in a secret passage?"

"It's fun," he said. "The great designers always find a way to surprise you."

He took her hand to cross the study, and she felt a thrill ripple up her arm. The immediate chemistry when they met was turning into a deeper attraction. It was one thing to admire a handsome man, and another to enjoy being with him. With Nick, she had both.

Taking her shoulders, he placed her in front of a circular iron staircase that ascended three stories high. Surrounding the stairs on every side were books, all of them easily within reach. "This is the library."

"I love it."

Kelly was a reader. During the long hours when her clients were in labor, it was always handy to have a book. Though she used a digital tablet for convenience, she preferred the feel of printed pages in her hand.

She scampered up the stairs, pausing to pull out titles that ranged from nonfiction biography to poetry to the latest thrillers. "It's so neat and compact. I usually have half-read books spilling all over my house. When I packed up my stuff in Texas, I had boxes and boxes of books."

"You could always donate them," he said, "or recycle."

"Recycle? I couldn't do that to my books." She dramatically grasped her heart. "You might as well ask me to let a box of puppies get ground up into mulch."

They shared a grin. Was it a mistake to get so friendly? She might run the risk of turning into his gal pal, and that wasn't the role she wanted.

"What do you think of Julia?" he asked.

Her honest opinion wasn't too flattering. Though she'd been touched by Julia's need to know that her lover was thinking of her in his last moments, Kelly had also been turned off by her anger. "This probably isn't the best time to meet her."

"She's a difficult person to get close to."

"Not many friends?"

"Why would you think that?" he asked.

"Nobody's here to comfort her. When someone close to you dies, friends usually show up with casseroles and flowers. At the very least, I'd expect her children to be here."

"We're lucky they're not. Her daughter is

okay, but her son, Arthur, is a jerk and a con man."

She stood on the staircase a few steps higher than Nick and gazed down at him. It was an unusual perspective. He was so tall that she'd gotten used to looking up. "We should get back to Julia."

"I'll help you down."

His large hands grasped just above her waist, and he lifted her effortlessly. She hadn't been expecting his touch. Being this close to him nearly took her breath away. As he slid her down the length of his body, the tiny thrill she'd felt earlier spread through her and turned into an earthquake.

He took her hand again as they left the library. His grip was totally masculine, slightly calloused. He'd told her that he worked construction on some of his projects. Seeing him in a tool belt with his shirt off would be a real treat.

They returned to the sofa and chairs in front

of the fireplace. Their timing was excellent; Julia was just coming from the kitchen with a teapot and cookies on a tray. Reluctantly, Kelly released his hand and sat on the sofa.

While Nick added four lumps of sugar to his tea, he asked, "Do you know what Samuel was working on?"

"He hasn't been doing much lately."

"But you said he was traveling. Where did he go?"

"I'm not sure. He hasn't turned in receipts or travel vouchers." She gave an annoyed snort. "Not that your uncle ever concerned himself with paying the bills and managing the money."

Kelly winced inside. If Julia was irritated by a couple of missing receipts, she was going to be outraged about the million-dollar debt.

"To be frank," Julia said as she primly sipped her tea, "I'm the one who has been busy. Marian Whitman has me going over old accounts, looking for payables that haven't been collected.

The way she acts, you'd think Spencer Enterprises was going bankrupt."

"Samuel had a special project," Nick said, "one that required special financing. Does anything come to mind?"

"Come to think of it, I saw a few charges on his company credit card for the Hearthstone Motel. I didn't know exactly where it was, but I recognized the name, Hearthstone. It's that little town near the Valiant gold mine."

"Can you think of any reason why he'd go there?"

She set down her tea and aimed a harsh glare on Nick. "Stop beating around the bush. Tell me what you know, and I'll try to fill in the blanks."

Nick laid it out for her. "Samuel borrowed a million dollars."

"That can't be true." Her chin drew back like a turtle going into its shell. "I take care of the money, and he never mentioned it to me. A million dollars?"

"You're saying that you never deposited that money."

"Oh, Nick, you're so like your uncle, as irresponsible as the day is long. Neither of you have a clue about how finance works. A million dollars isn't something you take to the bank, sign on the back and put into an account. There are procedures."

"I'm aware of that." His jaw tensed, and Kelly could tell that he was annoyed by being described as irresponsible. "A million-dollar liability would have to go through Marian and the attorneys. But this time, it didn't. Samuel handled the transaction himself."

"Disaster," she muttered.

"I want to know why he needed the money. He had to be starting a new project of some kind, maybe some kind of housing development near the gold mine."

"You work in the mountains," she said. "Why wouldn't he talk to you about it? Wait, I know the answer. A million-dollar housing development in a depressed area is an absurd concept, even for Samuel."

Kelly didn't understand the housing market the way Nick and Julia did, but it was common knowledge that mountain housing wasn't selling well right now. There weren't a lot of permanent jobs in the mountain towns, and the average buyer didn't want to commute when gas prices were so high. On the other hand, the multimillion-dollar dwellings in the high-class ski resorts always seemed to find buyers.

"Maybe it wasn't a development," she suggested. "On the drive here, Nick told me about Thornewood Castle and Heart Island. Samuel might have contracted to build one huge, fabulous house."

"In which case," Julia said, "the buyer would put up the money."

"Kelly has a point," Nick said, coming to her rescue. "Samuel might have been doing a fantastic house on spec. You know that's possible, Julia. He's done things like that before."

She stood and paced across the room to the fireplace. A splash of red through the stained glass gave a burst of color to her bland, shapeless outfit. Kelly thought the red matched Julia's angry mood. She didn't like being left out of the loop, especially when it came to dollars and cents.

"You said Samuel negotiated himself," she said. "How did he convince anyone to give him the cash?"

"He used the Valiant gold as collateral."

This bit of information seemed to upset her more than anything else. Julia actually stamped her foot. "Is there any danger that the loan is valid and the gold could be lost?"

"We'll find out next week," Nick said. "I've promised to pay back Samuel's obligation. If I don't make the payment, the lender has a valid claim."

"And who is this idiot who negotiated with Samuel?"

"I've met the man, and he's not stupid. His name is Barry Radcliff."

"Radcliff?" Julia threw her hands in the air. "The more you tell me, the worse this gets."

"How do you know him?"

"Not from reputable business dealings," she said archly. "I'm familiar with his reputation for destroying the environment. He's opposed to the current legislation to limit fracking in the oil business. Years ago, he was involved with some of the early strip-mining projects on the western slope, and it was rumored that he used the roughnecks who worked for him like a gang of thugs."

If Kelly had heard that profile before Nick went into the limo, she would have dialed 911 immediately. Radcliff sounded dangerous.

Nick stood. "You understand my concern. Radcliff isn't going to be a pussycat when it comes to collecting the debt. We stand to lose a big chunk of the Valiant gold."

She repeated, "Disaster."

When they took their leave, the goodbyes between Julia and Nick were strained. They hadn't actually argued, but Julia was angry about what Samuel had done.

At the door, Nick turned back toward her. "I hate to leave you here alone. Is there anybody I can call?"

"I'll be all right." She sounded defensive. "I'm accustomed to being alone."

In the SUV, Kelly asked, "What did she mean about being alone? She made it sound like your uncle didn't live with her."

"He didn't."

"But they were lovers."

"You know how some couples need to sleep in separate beds because they toss and turn too much? Julia and my uncle needed separate houses because she's a neat freak, and he was a slob."

It was none of her business to criticize another couple's living arrangements. The only time she'd lived with a man was during her marriage to Ted, and that had been a mess. "I'll bet Samuel's house is pretty spectacular."

"You'd be wrong. He never really settled into one place. He moves in, starts renovating and when he's done, the house sells. For the past year, he's lived in a condo."

The road leading from Julia's twisted through the secluded, secretive forest. At the intersection with the main road, they had a wide panoramic view of the valley and the little town of Valiant nestled below. To the south, she could see the distinctive outline of the Flatirons.

"Do you think Samuel's project had something to do with the gold mine?" she asked.

"It's a place to start." He glanced over toward her. "But first, we're going to check with the investigator who works for Spencer Enterprises and see what we can find out about Trask."

The visit to Julia's house had pushed her concerns about Trask out of her mind. Compared to

Radcliff and the million dollars, he was nothing more than a blip.

At least she hoped so.

# Chapter Seven

*Monday, 4:15 p.m.*

"Radcliff is a cold-blooded killer." Rod Esterhauser slammed the flat of his hand on the surface of Nick's desk in his office on the tenth floor of the Spencer Building.

"Has he ever been charged?" Nick asked in a low, calm voice. His strategy with the longtime head attorney for Spencer Enterprises was to maintain control and play his cards close to the vest. Otherwise, they'd both be yelling.

"Guys like Radcliff don't get charged," Rod said. "They hire henchmen and minions."

"And attorneys who play beach volleyball."

"What?" Rod's voice went up a few decibels. "What the hell are you talking about?"

In his effort to avoid engaging in argument, Nick kept his back turned to the attorney. He stood at the window with Kelly beside him. As he looked down at her shining hair, he had the urge to slip his arm around her shoulders, which probably wouldn't be considered appropriate, but would definitely keep his attention focused somewhere other than on Rod Esterhauser.

He turned his gaze to the foothills where the long shadows of dusk were beginning to settle. His office was directly above his uncle's and had the best view in the ten-story building.

As he turned to face Rod Esterhauser, Nick prepared to dig in his heels. "We're going to honor the loan to Radcliff. The document appears to be in order."

"This document?" Rod waved the single piece of paper. "I could tear this thing apart in court."

"But you won't."

Rod Esterhauser was a stocky man with short,

bristling gray hair. Though he wasn't a cowboy and probably hadn't been on a horse in years, he preferred Western-cut suits and bolo ties. Right now, his face was red from shouting.

"Is this about the gold?" he asked. "Are you scared to take a risk with the Valiant gold?"

Nick looked down at the surface of his desk. Since he didn't really spend much time in this office, there was a minimum of clutter—a photo of his daughters and a couple of knick-knacks. He had the sense that something was missing.

"I'm not scared, Rod. I'll pay off the loan because that's what my uncle would want me to do. There was a time, not so long ago, that Spencer Enterprises made deals with nothing more than a handshake."

"Before the economy went straight to hell and housing starts dropped into the—"

"Either Spencer Enterprises pays the loan," Nick said, "or I'll cover it myself."

"Is that so? Do you really think you can come up with a million in cash by next week?"

"You bet I can," he said with more confidence than was justified. Most of his assets were tied up in property and investments.

Rod shook his head. "Marian isn't going to like this. And neither is your brother. Jared gets back on Friday, you know."

"My mind is made up," Nick said. "There are other topics we need to talk about. What's going on with the investigation into Samuel's death?"

"So far, the police are calling it suicide. The forensics team didn't find any unusual prints or trace evidence to suggest that Samuel was murdered."

Nick wasn't so sure. "It doesn't seem right."

"I've got to agree with you." The wind went out of him. Rod visibly shrank as he sat in the chair opposite the desk. "Your uncle and I had plenty of scuffles, but I always liked the feisty old guy. He didn't seem like somebody who'd kill himself. Or leave a note saying he was sorry."

Nick looked over toward Kelly. She stood in

front of his bookcase with her head tilted sideways to read the titles. Her position reminded him of how excited she'd been when she saw Julia's library. She bent at the waist and picked up something on the floor.

Coming toward his desk, she held up a chunk of pyrite. "What's this?"

"It's fool's gold." That's what had been missing from his desk. He placed the rock beside the photo of his kids and moved on to the next order of business. "What have you found out about Trask?"

"Who?"

"The fake private investigator who approached Kelly."

"O'Shea is taking care of that." Rod took his cell phone from his pocket. "I'll call him for a progress report."

Kelly touched the sleeve of Nick's jacket to get his attention. "If it'd help, I can sit down with a sketch artist."

"I think they do composite sketches on computer now."

"I'll do whatever I can, and then I need to leave. I can call Serena to pick me up."

He still had concerns about her safety. "Trask could be part of a bigger problem. It might be good for you to stay somewhere else."

"Of course, I will," she immediately agreed. "If there's any chance of danger, I don't want Serena's family involved. But I don't want to cause a lot of extra trouble, either. Do you think there's a threat?"

"I hope not."

Rod snapped his cell phone closed and leaned back in his chair. "O'Shea is on his way up here."

Still worried about Kelly, Nick moved on to the next issue to discuss with Rod. "When we drove up to the building, I saw a television news truck parked at the curb."

"The Spencer family is news. Everybody from the governor on down knew your uncle."

Rod laced his fingers over his belly. "I called in security. They're keeping the media out of the building and watching your sister-in-law's house. By the way, you might want to have a little chitchat with Lauren. She's pretty upset, and being pregnant doesn't help."

Nick wasn't surprised by the media attention. His family was a big deal in Colorado. Reporters and photographers had covered his wedding, the birth of his kids and his divorce. Most recently, he'd been featured in a magazine article about the state's most eligible bachelors.

Craig O'Shea rushed into Nick's office. With his shaggy red hair, jeans and baggy sweater, he looked more like a hip snowboarder than a hard-nosed private investigator. He claimed that his casual appearance was a disguise. People didn't mind talking to him. They opened up and gave him information.

He closed the door. Clearly excited, he turned to them and announced, "I've got new evidence."

"Hold on there," Rod said. "First we want to hear about Trask."

"Really?" He walked two paces toward the desk and then went back to the door. "This evidence changes everything."

"It'll keep. First, Trask."

"Okay, sure, I can give you that info real quick. I couldn't find anything on Y. E. Trask. I mean nothing at all, zero, zip, *nada*. He's not listed with any professional organizations, and nobody else has ever heard of him." He'd been talking so fast that his words overlapped. He paused to take a breath. "The good news is that I checked in criminal records, and he's not in that database. The bad news is that I couldn't even find a driver's license."

"I can describe him," Kelly said. "He has white hair."

"Already have that description. He's not an albino, is he?"

"No, it's prematurely gray. I'd guess that he's only in his thirties." She dug into her purse.

"And I have his business card. Can you get fingerprints off that?"

"I can try." O'Shea took the card from her, holding it by the edges. "Don't count on getting a positive identification. Real life isn't like those forensics TV shows. Okay, are we done with Trask?"

"Not yet." Nick wasn't ready to let this go. "It must mean something that you can't find any information on him."

"Simple conclusion." O'Shea deposited the card in a clear plastic bag he took from his jean's pocket. "Y. E. Trask is a fake name."

"Can we tell who he works for?"

"Do you have somebody in mind?"

"Barry Radcliff." If Trask was one of the minions or henchmen that Rod was worried about, Kelly might be in danger.

"I'll check it out." O'Shea's gaze darted around the room. His new evidence must be really significant. He looked as if he was jumping out of his skin.

"Tell us," Nick said.

"The autopsy report. It's amazing that we have results already. Rod said he'd pull some strings, but I'm impressed, and so was the medical examiner."

"What did they find?" Nick asked.

"I'll show you."

O'Shea pulled Nick out from behind his desk and had him stand beside it. He pointed to the floor. "He fell here, right?"

"Yes." Nick's voice was terse. He didn't want to reimagine that scene.

"And the blood was here. Not tracked all over the room."

"That's correct."

"According to the autopsy report, the path of the bullet indicated a slightly upward trajectory." Using his index finger to represent the barrel of a gun, O'Shea pointed to the right side of Nick's body. "If Samuel committed suicide, the weapon would have been approximately here, and then fired."

Nick's interest was aroused. "If he committed suicide? I thought that was a given."

"Maybe not," O'Shea said. "The autopsy showed that the bullet went up. That's not the natural path for someone shooting at himself. Your hand would point down."

"Not necessarily." Nick swallowed hard. Imagining his uncle killing himself was painful. "He could have aimed up."

"Try it." O'Shea stepped back. "Pretend you're pointing a gun at yourself."

Nick held up his right hand, but he didn't need to aim it. He had the answer already. "Samuel was murdered."

Rod Esterhauser shook his head. "I don't get it."

"My uncle was left-handed."

He should have realized last night that he'd taken the weapon from Samuel's right hand. They'd wasted a day of valuable investigative time. Nick didn't know how the murderer had gotten away without being seen. And he didn't know the motive. But he was 100 percent certain that his uncle had been killed.

This changed everything.

KELLY WAS ANXIOUS TO GO HOME to Serena's farm. The chaos of meandering goats and llamas and kids would be a welcome relief from an investigation that had gone into high gear with a combination of police detectives, CBI agents and more forensic researchers. She was glad that many of them wore jackets with the initials of their department on the back, allowing her to identify their jobs.

Nick stood in the eye of this storm. Though he never raised his voice or was unreasonable, he was the unacknowledged leader. Nobody was required to salute him or call him "sir," but they looked to him for guidance, and so did she. She'd promised Nick that she wouldn't leave until O'Shea had more information on Trask.

In Nick's office, she sat quietly, watching

and waiting as the minutes ticked slowly by. It was her nature to be patient, but time dragged. When she looked through the window, she was surprised to see that it wasn't yet nightfall.

Nick approached her and sat in the chair beside her. "Bored?"

"I wish there was something I could do to help. With all this activity swirling around, I feel like a bump on a log that's stuck in the middle of the river. All I can do is watch."

"According to O'Shea's sources, Trask is still the invisible man. Nobody knows of a white-haired guy who works for Radcliff or anybody else."

"Is that more or less dangerous?"

"It's always better to know what we're dealing with," he said. "I can arrange for you to stay with me tonight. Or you could go back to the house with Lauren. We have a security team there."

"I'm not one to take risks," she said, "especially not if it means Serena and her family could be in danger. But I can't help thinking that Trask already has everything he needs from me."

"How so?"

"Since we now believe that your uncle was murdered, it makes sense for Trask to contact me. He'd want to know if Samuel named his killer before he died."

"Is this theory supposed to reassure me?" His eyebrows lifted. "If he was looking for the name, Trask has to be working for the murderer."

"Okay, he's a bad guy. But he knows I'm not a threat."

He took her hand. This time, it was more than a friendly gesture. His fingers caressed hers. "I want you to be safe, Kelly. If anything happened to you, I couldn't live with myself."

Deep inside, she responded to his sincerity and concern. He cared for her. It had been a long time since anybody wanted to protect her, maybe never, and she liked the feeling of warmth and safety. Going home with him appealed to her on many different levels, but she didn't think it was necessary.

"I'll stay with Serena tonight," she said.

"Okay. Lauren showed up a little while ago. She can drive you."

"Why is Lauren here? We don't have Lamaze class until tomorrow night."

"She's upset about something." Nick cringed. "I'm sure we'll hear all about it."

It took only a few minutes to locate Lauren on the ninth floor outside Marian Whitman's office, ticking off a list of complaints on her fingers. The thin blond accountant was utterly motionless. Kelly had never seen such a display of willpower. Marian's face could have been a Kabuki mask that registered no emotion whatsoever.

When Lauren stopped talking, Marian said simply, "Are you done?"

Hands on hips, Lauren glared. "I just told you

seven things I need help with. You're not going to do a damn thing about it, are you?"

"Arrangements for Samuel Spencer's funeral and memorial are outside the purview of my job," Marian said. "I am well aware that you are the wife of the CEO. But if Jared were here, he would tell me that the way I can help is to keep my focus on Spencer Enterprises business."

Nick stepped between the two women. "Problem?"

"You bet," Lauren said. "Ever since early this morning, I've been getting phone calls. Flower arrangements have been arriving. Relatives want me to arrange to pick them up at the airport, and they all want to stay at the house."

"You've got two people on staff," he said.

"A housekeeper and a part-time cook. If I was throwing a dinner party, I'd be all set. This is a hundred times more complicated. Don't even get me started about the media."

Lauren's breathing became more rapid. She flung out an arm to brace herself against the wall. Kelly had spent enough time with pregnant women to know that stress was a problem. "This isn't good for you," she said.

"Tell me about it."

"I have an idea." It wasn't Kelly's place to make suggestions, but this seemed like a perfect solution. "You should call Julia Starkey and ask her to help. Nobody knew Samuel better than Julia, and I've heard that she's very efficient."

Lauren stared at her for two seconds, then she burst into a huge smile. "That's perfect."

"I'll make the call," Nick said. "I'll bet Julia will be glad to have something to do."

"Perfect," Lauren repeated. She whipped around to face Marian. "Why didn't you think of that?"

"Come with me, Lauren." Nick ushered his sister-in-law away from the accountant, which seemed like a really good idea. If Marian ever lost control, it might be terrifying. "You can thank Kelly by giving her a ride back to Serena's place.

Then you go home, put your feet up and wait for Julia."

On the elevator to the ground floor, Kelly focused on Lauren's health. "This is an important time in your pregnancy. You need to remember to eat, drink plenty of water and not get overtired. Put your needs first."

"I'm so glad I ran into you." She gave her a clumsy hug. "Nick, aren't you glad?"

"Blissful."

"I'm parked in front," Lauren said. "That means we're going to have to walk past a bunch of media people."

Kelly's stomach twisted. Her ex-husband had been expert at courting the media and giving them opportunities to capture his gorgeous face in video or in photos. She had despised the attention. Society-page photos had provided Ted with another opportunity to critique her wardrobe. Once she'd tripped and fallen in front of a television camera. It hadn't been pretty.

She glanced at Nick. "Is there another way out?"

"It's no big deal," Lauren assured her. "Give them a 'no comment' and move on."

Before she could voice another objection, Kelly was out of the building. Leading with her pregnant belly, Lauren plowed through the reporters. In contrast, Kelly tried to be invisible. She hunched her shoulders and leaned close to Nick, instinctively seeking his protection as the light from a TV camera flared. A couple of reporters with microphones came at them, repeating Nick's name over and over to get him to look at them.

The most persistent reporter got close enough to ask a question. "Was it murder or suicide? Hey, Nick, can we get a quote?"

As Nick pushed past them, the reporter stared at Kelly. For a moment their eyes met.

"I know you," said the man with the microphone. "I've seen you before."

She avoided his gaze as she reached out and

touched the door of Lauren's SUV. She had almost escaped…almost.

The reporter crowed, "You're Ted Maxwell's ex-wife."

Busted.

# Chapter Eight

*Tuesday, 1:15 p.m.*

Rather than spending her entire day hiding at Serena's farm, Kelly had decided to take action. In addition to the five women in her Lamaze class, Serena's client list included eight other expectant mothers and four who had given birth in the past couple of months. Kelly's plan was to introduce herself while at the same time getting more familiar with the area. With her van loaded and ready to roll, she set out on her quest.

The morning had been mostly uneventful. She'd taken four calls from Nick giving her updates, none of which were particularly earth-shaking. Otherwise, she was removed from the Spencer Building and all the troubles associated with the investigation that the media had reduced to a simple headline: Murder or Suicide?

On the evening and morning news, one of the television channels had run the video showing her and Nick rushing from the Spencer Building. She looked like a frightened rabbit, but she hadn't been identified as the ex-wife of Ted Maxwell, which meant this wasn't the most embarrassing thing that had ever happened to her.

Using her GPS map, she found the secluded mountain cabin of a client who had given birth two months ago. The woman was ecstatic to have company. Her health and that of her infant son were good, but she was concerned about the possibility of postpartum depression. Kelly listened carefully to her symptoms and referred her to a therapist that Serena had on a list of recommended professionals. At the same time, she strongly suggested that the new mother and baby spend more time outside, getting involved with other people. With the winter weather giving way to spring, it would be a lot easier to escape the isolated cabin.

From there, she drove into Valiant and popped into Roxanne's beauty shop. The bustling atmosphere in the salon was the opposite of the quiet surrounding the mountain cabin. She managed to get Roxanne away from her well-meaning stylists for a few private words, and learned that she'd been more exhausted than usual, too tired to cook dinner for her husband. Kelly didn't even have to say her advice out loud. Roxanne knew that she was driving herself too hard to get everything done before the baby came.

As she stepped out onto the main street that ran through the middle of Valiant, Kelly paused to enjoy the weather. With the temperature in the mid-sixties with very little wind, it was just warm enough to be comfortable with a light jacket or sweater. On the opposite side of the street, she noticed a man leaning against a building and holding a newspaper that he wasn't really reading. The "Murder or Suicide?" heading wasn't what caught her attention. He seemed to be looking directly at her, as though he'd been waiting for her to appear. He folded his paper and got into a white sedan that was parked on the street.

Had he been watching for her? She took out her cell phone, thinking that she should call Nick and tell him, but he had enough to worry about without her getting all paranoid.

After she made another two stops and got back into her van, she looked into the rearview mirror and saw the white sedan following her. Was it a coincidence? There were a lot of white cars on the road. She drove into the parking lot for the supermarket and angled around until she had a clear view of the driver. It was the same man. His sedan turned right and headed in another direction.

Cruising past the parking lot was a stretch limo with tinted windows. There was no mistaking that vehicle. Barry Radcliff was in town. The driver didn't stop. Had Radcliff been looking for her? That made no sense at all.

Checking her wristwatch, she saw that the afternoon was almost over. After one more stop, she'd head over to the Spencer Building for her class at six. Last on her list was Daisy, the fresh-faced woman who kept everything organic. Her home on the outskirts of Valiant looked like a model for organic living with a new baby. She happily showed Kelly the guest bedroom that she'd converted into a birthing room with soothing colors and a sophisticated sound system, created by her husband, the engineer.

Daisy's enthusiasm rubbed off on Kelly and lifted her spirits. By the time she left the house, she'd decided that there was a plausible explanation for Radcliff's limo to be in Valiant. Clearly, he had other business.

As she drove away from Daisy's house, the white sedan pulled around the corner. The man who had been watching her had picked up a passenger. She caught a glimpse of his white hair. It was Trask.

She couldn't dismiss her fears. She was being stalked.

Her fingers clenched on the steering wheel. What did these people want with her? Until two days ago, she'd never even met the Spencers. She'd never known Uncle Samuel.

Windows up and doors locked, she drove to the Spencer Building. Every car she passed seemed like a threat. When someone honked, she nearly jumped out of her skin. To avoid the media who were still gathered near the front entrance, she went to the underground parking garage. A mistake? Anybody who watched thrillers knew that bad things happened in enclosed parking lots.

She grabbed her satchel from the back of her van, made a mad dash to the exit and raced up the staircase. Within seconds, she'd rushed into the building. It was almost five o'clock, and the people who worked here were leaving. Having lots of witnesses was a good thing.

After ordering her coffee, she called Nick on her cell phone and told him she was downstairs on the ground floor.

He picked up on the tension in her voice. "Are you okay?"

"I don't want you to worry," she said, "but I think I might have picked up a stalker."

"I'll be right there."

She took a seat at a round table in the central atrium. When she lifted the cardboard coffee cup to her lips, her hand was shaking. The hairs on the back of her neck prickled, and she looked over her shoulder. Was he here?

Nick strode toward her from the elevator, and she'd never been more relieved to see someone. As soon as he sat at her table, she started talking, telling him about the man on the street and Radcliff's limo and the sighting of Trask.

"Did you get a license plate number?"

"I should have," she said. "I didn't think of

it. This is kind of new to me. I've never been stalked before."

"Is there anything else you can tell me about the guy?"

"He was average height and weight. Nothing remarkable about him at all, other than he was lurking around and following me." She leaned back in her chair. Being with Nick was already curing her panic. "I really only saw the guy three times, but then I saw the limo. It felt like they were swarming around me like a bunch of sharks and I was a helpless minnow."

"Don't be scared, little minnow. I won't let anything bad happen to you."

He pulled his cell phone from the inner pocket of his gray tweed sports jacket. The slim phone looked tiny in his calloused hand, but he used it like a lethal weapon. His confidence made her believe that he was capable of dealing with any threat. She sighed and said, "Thank you."

"For what? Getting you into this mess?"

It had been a very long time since anyone

offered to take care of her and meant it. Sure, she had friends like Serena, and her family in Chicago, but she didn't have a partner who was on her side no matter what, even when she was wrong.

Picking up her coffee and her satchel, she stood and said, "I should get upstairs to the gym before the couples arrive for class. Coming with me?"

"After I make a couple of calls."

"Please don't be late," she said. "I don't think Lauren could stand any more disruption of her schedule."

"She's doing a lot better today. Having Julia come over to help made all the difference. She's got everything on track—obituaries, arrangements for a memorial service, plans for cremation, notifications, everything."

Glancing toward the hall that led to the bank of elevators, she said, "Too bad I have to go all the way to the front to go up one floor. With this high ceiling atrium, it almost seems like there should be a staircase to the second floor."

"At one time, there was. We took it out to provide better security for the upper floors. The same is true for the underground parking. There's no elevator from the parking levels."

"Because of the gold?"

"A little." When he stood, he towered over her in a most pleasant way. "Mostly, we upped our level of security because that's standard procedure for office buildings, even if all we're protecting is software and sportswear."

"Sports?"

"There's an office for a national distributor of sports equipment on the sixth and seventh floors. We should stop by and visit them. What's your favorite outdoor activity? Skiing?"

"I do a little cross-country," she said, "but I really love rock climbing."

He grinned. "You're not afraid of heights."

"I like tall places." *And tall men,* she thought.

"But I tend to get kind of freaked out when weird cars and limos start tailing my van."

He rested his hand on her shoulder and gently stroked her arm. "No freak-outs necessary. I've got it covered."

"Don't be late for class."

As she strolled toward the elevators, her attitude was completely transformed from earlier when she'd been looking over her shoulder and expecting something terrible to sneak up on her. No longer alone, she had Nick watching her back. It felt good to trust him.

In the gym classroom that was separate from the rest of the gymnasium and the exercise equipment, she moved the chairs out of the way, set out mats and waited for her class. They were all punctual, even Nick, who stepped through the door at exactly one minute until six o'clock. He gave her a wink and took his place beside his sister-in-law.

After a brief question-and-answer session, she concentrated on the breathing techniques. As

Kelly inhaled and exhaled in the distinctive Lamaze patterns, alternating quick panting and deep gulps of oxygen, her tension abated. *Always remember to breathe*. It was a good lesson for her to keep in mind.

Having Nick so close was another deterrent to stress. When she caught a glimpse of his bemused grin or his blue eyes, warmth spread through her body. Not exactly a soothing sensation, the heat he generated inside her was too exciting—exciting in a good way. This man might be the best antidote to all her self-doubt and frustration.

The class was over before she knew it. The couples left, and Kelly was left in the gym classroom with Nick and Lauren. As they rearranged the classroom to look the way it had when Kelly entered, Lauren thanked her for the suggestion of calling Julia.

"She's so organized," Lauren said, "and she knows everything about Samuel and what he would have wanted."

"I'm glad it's working out," Kelly said.

To her surprise, tears appeared in Lauren's eyes. "Oh, honey, I'm so sorry. If you need to talk, call me. I can't imagine how embarrassed you must be. What that bastard did to you is awful, just plain awful."

Which bastard was that? She struggled free from the restricting embrace. "I have no idea what you're talking about."

"You don't know?" Lauren's face squinched. "I don't want to be the one to tell you."

"Don't worry. I promise not to shoot the messenger."

"It's that reporter who recognized you last night," Lauren said. "He has a blog."

Kelly's warm, relaxed attitude turned ice cold. "He said something about me and Ted."

"Your ex is running for office. He's in the news a lot." Lauren winced. "You should read it for yourself."

"You're right." She pivoted and faced Nick. "Take me to the nearest computer with internet."

She should have anticipated trouble, should have known that she couldn't sit back and relax. Her past would always catch up with her. She and Nick left Lauren and took the elevator to his tenth-floor office.

Calmly, he said, "Are you sure you want to do this?"

"It's better to know."

Lauren might be exaggerating. How bad could the blog be? She and Ted had gotten divorced, which was no big deal. Marriages ended every day. Their lawyers had argued over possessions but it hadn't been a bloody fight. She'd given up almost everything but walked away with a healthy cash settlement. There hadn't been a custody battle....

She swallowed hard, fearing that her darkest secret was about to become public knowledge, revealed on a blog. The real reason she'd ended her marriage to Ted was that she'd had a miscarriage. The memory still hurt. Kelly had been in her first trimester. They hadn't told anyone that she was pregnant.

She'd been at work, felt a cramp and then…it had happened so quickly. Her ob-gyn saw her as an outpatient, didn't even admit her. Physically, she wasn't in bad shape at all. Emotionally, she was destroyed.

Having a baby was her most cherished dream. As soon as she'd gotten the positive sign on an early pregnancy test, she'd started making plans, thinking of names, imagining the wonderful ways her life would change. She was going to be a mother.

Ted hadn't been enthusiastic when she told him. He kept saying that they should wait, there was plenty of time for children, but she knew that as soon as he saw the baby he'd change his mind. He'd love their child. Their marriage would take on new life.

When she'd told him about the miscarriage, he hadn't been able to hide his relief. He'd told her it just wasn't meant to be, and they'd be more

careful in the future to avoid unwanted preg-
nancies. Unwanted? Having a baby was everything to her.

Her tears offended him. Her grief made him
angry.

She took off two days and went into the mountains where she found a peaceful glen near a
rushing stream. In a rosewood box, she buried
the baby blanket her grandmother had given her
to be used for her firstborn. As she wept beside
the grave, she knew her marriage was over. She
and Ted were too different.

Her feet felt like lead as she trudged through
the tenth floor of Spencer Enterprises toward
Nick's office. She didn't want to relive the pain
of her miscarriage. What kind of horrible spin
could a blogger put on her personal tragedy?
And how would he know? The miscarriage
wasn't something she talked about, not with
anyone. And she was fairly sure that Ted hadn't
mentioned their child.

Nick unlocked the door to his office and held

it for her. She shuffled inside and took a seat in a chair beside his desk. Her gaze rested on the double photo of his two daughters, laughing girls with black hair and eyes as blue as their father's.

It took Nick only a moment to fire up his laptop and locate the blog. After only a glance, he turned the screen toward her.

The photograph showed her with Nick leaving the Spencer Building. The header said Better Luck This Time?

The first paragraph read, "Kelly Evans, the former Mrs. Ted Maxwell, has hooked up with well-known bachelor Nick Spencer, whose uncle's death remains a mystery. Let's hope Kelly has better luck this time. Her marriage to Maxwell ended when it was revealed that he had a mistress and had been sleeping with his paralegal."

She hadn't known.

# Chapter Nine

*Tuesday, 7:11 p.m.*

For a moment, Kelly thought she was going to pass out. Her spine turned to jelly. Spots danced behind her eyelids. Her throat pinched closed. *Remember to keep breathing.* She gasped loudly. "Water."

Nick dashed from the office. As soon as he was gone, she wondered if she should take this unsupervised opportunity to leap from the chair, barricade the door and stay here for, say, the next twelve years or so. Could her life possibly be more humiliating? Her ex had been having an affair. Worse, he had a mistress. Even worse, she hadn't known. Sure, she'd suspected there might be something going on with the cute little paralegal in his office. What was her name? Cheryl, her name was Cheryl, and she seemed like such a nice person. Kelly groaned. She'd sent flowers—supposedly from Ted, of course—on cute little Cheryl's birthday.

Nick returned with a coffee mug, half-filled with water. "Here."

She took a couple of sips and looked up at him. "I wish this was poisonous hemlock."

"No, you don't."

"Maybe a sleeping potion that would knock me out until this blows over. How long will that be? Is there a time limit for feeling like an idiot?"

"There's nothing wrong with you." He leaned down to her eye level. "Your ex is the jerk."

"Why do men cheat?"

"Not all men do."

"Did you? Is that why your marriage broke up?" As soon as the words left her mouth, she regretted them. "Forget I said that. It's none of my business."

"You've got a mouth on you when you're angry."

The last thing she wanted was to insult him, the first man she'd trusted in years. "I'm sorry."

"Don't be. I'm glad to see that you're not all sunshine and sweetness." His stunning blue eyes regarded her with a steady, nonjudgmental calm. "To answer your question, I was faithful to my wedding vows, always faithful. And I tried as hard as I could to make the marriage work. But I couldn't be the man my ex-wife wanted."

She couldn't imagine Nick falling short in any category. Though she didn't want to pry, she already had her foot in her mouth. Might as well take another bite. "What did she expect from you?"

"Basically, she wanted me to be like my brother." He stood up straight and checked his wristwatch. "She wanted to be the wife of the

CEO, the queen of all things Spencer. And that's not my style. I hate corporate red tape. Being in the office five days a week gives me hives."

"You'd rather be an architect—the creative guy who draws up the plans."

"Not the man in a suit who cuts the ribbon at the launch of a new project," he said. "Our split was as friendly as a divorce can be, and we both love the kids."

"She's a good mom?"

"I've got no complaints. Hell, I even like her new husband. He runs an investment firm, and he's one rung away from the top job." He glanced at his watch again. "I don't want to rush you, but we have a logistics problem to work out."

"Logistics?" The shock of reading the blog was beginning to wear off, but she was still feeling the aftershocks. Her brain wasn't fully functional.

"You need protection," he said. "Until we know who's following you and why, you're not safe. That means you can't go back to Serena's tonight."

Even in her befuddled state, she understood what he was saying. "I think you're right about that."

"I'd like to have you stay with me at my condo. But you could also go to Lauren's house. She has plenty of room."

"I pick you." That was a no-brainer.

"Good choice." After he took the coffee mug from her and placed it on the desktop, he grasped both her hands and pulled her to her feet. "I have an appointment in ten minutes. Either I can arrange for someone to take you to my place or you can come with me. The appointment is with Barry Radcliff."

"What? How did you—"

"He's the person I called before the Lamaze class. There weren't any other options. Nobody answers the Trask phone number, and we don't have an identity for the other guy."

Coming face-to-face with Radcliff—a man

who had been described as a stone-cold killer—was intimidating, but she was curious about him and his slinky brunette attorney, and she figured nothing bad would happen to her if she was with Nick. "I'll stick with you."

"We should go now. He'll be waiting for us."

"In his limousine office?"

"Not this time."

"Good." She really hated limos.

ON THE WAY TO THE ELEVATOR, Nick placed his hand on Kelly's waist. The color had returned to her face, and her eyes were more focused. More than ever, he wanted to protect this woman. Her flash of temper reassured him; she wasn't completely defenseless. "We're going to have a nice dinner with Radcliff," he said.

"That's smart. There's nothing he can do in front of witnesses."

"He's not that kind of thug," Nick said. "If he meant to do us physical harm, he'd hire an expert. We'll have dinner, then we'll go to my place and relax."

She pushed a sweep of straight brownish-blond hair off her forehead. "Where are we going to eat?"

"The restaurant downstairs."

"The fancy place? With the 'haute cuisine'?"

"Don't let the tablecloths fool you. They grill a mean rib eye."

She stepped away from him. "I'm not dressed to go anyplace classy."

"Nobody's going to give you a hard time. It's my name on the building."

"And you look fine in your tweed jacket and jeans. I've been wearing these khakis all day. I'm a giant wrinkle." She looked down at the satchel she was carrying. "There's probably something in here that I can change into. At least I can put on fresh lipstick."

She darted into the ladies' room by the elevators.

"Five minutes," he called after her.

He leaned against the wall and folded his arms across his chest. Radcliff and his attorney would probably already be seated. Even though the restaurant was Spencer turf, arriving early gave Radcliff a slight edge in claiming the space, and their encounters were all about who was the boss.

Nick was glad to have another confrontation with Radcliff; it gave him a chance to probe for useful information about his uncle's death. All day long, he'd been playing the corporate game with Rod Esterhauser and Marian. The results were disappointing. The company accounts were in worse shape than he'd suspected, due to slow housing starts and even slower payouts on completed projects. If Jared didn't come back with a big, fat contract from the Singapore company that wanted to open a United States branch, they'd have to make drastic cuts and start letting employees go. He'd learned nothing new about Samuel.

Nobody knew what his uncle had been working on. They regarded him as a loose cannon, incapable of responsible financial decisions, which was fairly ironic because these same corporate people were delighted to point to Samuel's innovative and brilliant designs when selling Spencer Enterprises. His talent was one of their secret weapons, but they kept him out of their information loop and vice versa.

If Nick had been in town, the dynamic might have been different. He and Samuel were usually on the same page. The old man might have confided in him.

The police investigation was equally frustrating. In spite of the left-handed issue, they leaned toward suicide. Nick didn't agree. The more he thought about his uncle's death, the more he thought it was murder, an impossible murder.

Kelly emerged from the bathroom. She'd combed her hair, freshened her makeup and changed into a black leotard and tights that stopped at her ankles. Around her slender waist, she'd tied a long, silky scarf with a swirling pattern of black, gold and purple. On the left side, the fringed hem dipped past her knee. "You look damn good," he said.

She pushed back her hair to show dangling silver earrings. "I found these in the bottom of my bag. I was wearing them when I got called to help a woman in labor, stuck them in here and forgot about them. Lucky, huh?"

"That's a nice bag of tricks you have there."

"I take it with me when I get a call that someone is in labor. My medical stuff is in a different bag, but this one is sometimes more useful—it's full of bits and pieces that might come in handy, like the leotard and the shoes." She stuck out her foot so he could see her black cloth Chinese slippers.

"They're not bad. I like to see a woman in high heels. From an engineering standpoint, a heel does good things for the female form. But your form doesn't need any help. I'll say it again. You look damn good."

"Thank you."

Downstairs in the restaurant, the host showed them to a secluded table near the back where Radcliff and his attorney were waiting. The former volleyball player cleaned up good in an emerald-green silk blouse with a sparkly necklace and black pencil skirt. Radcliff looked uncomfortable in his suit and necktie, but he was gracious when he greeted Kelly.

She shook his hand and smiled sweetly. "I thought I saw your limousine earlier today."

"Maybe you did," Radcliff said. "I had business in Valiant."

Undeterred, she pushed her point. "It seemed that you were following me. Is there something you wanted to talk about?"

Radcliff nodded to Nick. "She's sharp, this one."

"And persistent," he said. "Might as well tell her the truth. Then we can move on."

The attorney spoke up. "Both statements are true. We had another appointment. When we identified Ms. Evans's van, we tracked her for a while, hoping she'd meet up with you, Nick, and we could get an update."

Radcliff gestured expansively. "Sit. Have some wine."

Nick held Kelly's chair for her. When she glanced up at him, he noticed the slender arch of her throat and the delicate hollow between her collarbones. Being with her was almost enough to make him forget the other reasons for talking to Radcliff—almost, but not entirely. He wanted to know the identity of the person Radcliff met with in Valiant today.

The Chardonnay was excellent, and Nick ordered another bottle to go with their shrimp appetizer. The restaurant was about half-full, and the atmosphere was low-key and pleasant. The conversation at their table flowed freely. The two women chatted about childbirth and career, a topic that required only an occasional nod from Nick and Radcliff. The only telling point was that Radcliff had five children and hadn't watched any of them being born. Squeamish?

That didn't sound like the vicious killer Rod Esterhauser described. It occurred to Nick that Rod might be building a wall between him and Radcliff.

Their main courses were served—steaks for Nick and the attorney, chicken for Kelly and a grilled-veggie salad for Radcliff, who was watching his cholesterol. After a few bites, Nick got down to business. "You mentioned that you wanted to see me. Why not just pick up the phone?"

"I wanted to be sure you'd take my call."

So he threatened Kelly? What kind of messed-up power play was that? "You've got my attention. What did you want?"

"It's no secret that your business is in financial hot water. I can help. I'll double the loan for six months. If you default, all the Valiant gold is mine."

"An interesting proposition," Nick said. One he definitely wouldn't take. "I have a few questions."

"Of course," said the attorney. Whenever the topic veered toward business, she stepped in. Very smooth.

"Since my uncle didn't run the money through the usual channels, no one knows what he did with it. We can't even verify that he received the cash."

"He insisted on a certain type of cashier's check," the attorney said. "I must admit that I was surprised. In this day of automatic transfer, the check seemed oddly old-fashioned."

"And untraceable," Nick said. "The money has already been drawn from your account, but there's no way of knowing what my uncle did with it."

That put Nick back to zero. He cut off a piece of rare steak and chewed slowly. Samuel might have hidden the check and never used it. He might have set up a whole new account, a whole new business and spent every penny.

"Another question," he said. "How did you meet my uncle?"

"He contacted me," Radcliff said. "He showed up at my place of business in Denver."

"Where's that?" Nick asked.

Before the attorney could stop him, Radcliff answered. "I keep an office on Blake Street, not far from the baseball stadium."

"What did my uncle say when he showed up?"

"He made the million-dollar proposition. Frankly, I was going to turn him down. I didn't have any reason to believe anything from this tall, goofy old guy." He paused. "Sorry, I didn't mean to insult him, God rest his soul."

"*Goofy* is accurate," Nick said. "What changed your mind about making the loan?"

"He brought me here and showed me the gold. I was hooked."

"It has that effect." Nick had only one more question. "You said you came to Valiant for a meeting. Are you in contact with anyone else from Spencer Enterprises?"

"Sorry, Nick." This time the attorney was

quick to stop her boss from replying. "We can't divulge our client list for you or anybody else."

They finished the meal with Nick promising to consider Radcliff's offer and to stay in touch. There was hostility between them with the threat of Radcliff taking the Valiant gold if he wasn't paid back, but their relationship was fairly sanguine.

Now came the good part of the evening. He'd been looking forward to time alone with Kelly. He tucked her into the passenger seat of his SUV and headed toward his condo. "What did you think of Radcliff?"

"He seemed old-fashioned in his attitudes and in the way he does business. I'm guessing that he's older than he looks, maybe in his sixties. He's smart to have that attorney with him at all times. Did you notice that she wasn't drinking? The lady stayed 100 percent alert."

"Do you think he had anything to do with my uncle's death?"

"I wouldn't be surprised. Radcliff is determined. And he wants that gold."

"I didn't believe him when he said he was following you to send me a message." Nick had already turned onto the street where his condo complex was located. His place was less than ten minutes away from the Spencer Building. "There's something else going on with him."

"I can't think of anyone being interested in me, other than for Samuel's last words."

Nick didn't want to bring this up, especially after her reaction to the blog, but another thought had occurred to him. "There's something about the timing. Why are these people following you now?"

"I don't know."

"Could it have anything to do with your ex-husband?"

# Chapter Ten

*Tuesday, 10:21 p.m.*

The anger and frustration she'd struggled to contain after reading the blog returned with the raging violence of a wildfire, tearing through her and destroying her self-control. She'd been followed. Because of her ex? If that was true, her past was tainting the present situation. Kelly hated to think that her poisonous marriage and divorce would affect anybody but her. She'd been humiliated. She'd been cheated on. And she had to deal with it. Nobody else had to be involved.

But her ex-husband's influence spread wide.

He was a public figure. He was making a run for a seat in the senate. His campaign ads showed him and his attractive, appropriately dressed new wife and their towheaded toddler, looking like the embodiment of the American dream.

An angry ex-wife didn't fit into that picture.

Nick parked his SUV in a numbered slot facing a landscaped hillside with three-story wood-sided buildings on each side. His condo complex wasn't the sort of upscale place where she'd expect a top executive to be living, and she was glad that Nick didn't need to be surrounded by luxury.

He came around the front of the SUV and opened her door. "My condo is on the third floor of the building on the right."

She unfastened her seat belt and stepped out. Through tight lips, she said, "This can't be about my ex. Trask never mentioned his name. And I don't think Radcliff gives a damn about him. But the stranger who was following me in Valiant might have been looking for a story about my divorce."

"Why wouldn't he talk to you?"

"I don't know."

"What was he looking for?"

"Scandal." Anger flared inside her. "He must be looking for a story."

Nick scanned the parking lot where nothing else was moving. "I didn't notice anyone following us tonight, but how will it look if you spend the night at my place?"

"Why would it matter? Neither of us is married. We're consenting adults." A horrible thought occurred to her. "Are you ashamed of being involved with someone like me?"

"God, no."

"That was the headline in the blog. Will I have better luck this time? That reporter already turned us into a couple." She didn't want to make his life more difficult than it already was. "You should take me somewhere else. A hotel? I can—"

Before she could finish the sentence, his mouth covered hers and stole her breath away. His firm lips pressed hard, demanding a response, and she gave herself over to their kiss, melting into his strong arms. Overwhelmed by a trembling sensation she hadn't felt in years, had maybe never truly experienced, she abandoned conscious thought. Every cell in her body yearned for the intense relief that comes with making love. She was desperate, driven by the fire that burned inside her. The night breeze swirled around them, and she was grateful for the cool that soothed those flames.

He ended the kiss but still held her against him. "You're not going to a hotel."

"It might be easier."

"I'm not looking for easy. I want someone real."

She buried her face against his chest and tightened her embrace. Closer, closer, she wanted to be so close that she was a part of him, and they were joined together. "Take me upstairs."

At the front entryway, he used his key to open the outer door. The carpeted foyer had an elevator and a staircase. The layout reminded her of a mountain condo where she and Ted had gone on a skiing vacation. Damn Ted Maxwell! Why was she thinking about him? Why wouldn't her memories of him shrivel up and die?

As she and Nick climbed the staircase, she paused on a landing to kiss him again. Her tongue plunged into his mouth. He tasted sweet and hot and slick. Her passion overwhelmed her regrets. Her needs were fierce and demanding. With Nick, she wasn't making a mistake. Her luck had changed for the better.

Unaware of anything but him, she ascended the rest of the stairs. By the time he unlocked the door to his condo, she could barely contain her desire. The inferno inside her consumed her thoughts and drove her to the brink.

As they tumbled into his condo, she was utterly unaware of her surroundings. Nothing existed but her need to make love to Nick. He was her salvation. When she felt his muscular arms holding her, she forgot everything else. She could lose herself in the blue of his eyes. He was the antidote to her memories.

Her hands became claws as she tore off his tweed jacket. Her eager fingers fumbled with the buttons on his shirt, and she plucked open one after another.

He caught her hands and held them, forcing her to slow down, and she moaned. She needed to touch his flesh and feel the beating of his heart against hers. He lightly kissed her forehead. He caressed her shoulders, sending shivers down her spine.

There was a time for gentleness, and this wasn't it. She wanted to be ravaged, to forget all the embarrassment and the hurt. The only thing that would quench the burning rage and humiliation inside her was fierce passion. *Fight fire with fire*. If she didn't make love to him right now, she would surely explode.

He whispered her name. "Are you all right?"

Hell, no, she wasn't all right. She was nearly insane. "Make love to me, Nick."

"You bet I will." But he took a backward step. "Let me take my time, to make love to you the way you deserve."

"Now," she said hoarsely as she threw her body against his. Her hand slid down his chest and lower until she grasped his rock-hard erection. "I know you want me."

He sucked in a breath. "Damn right I do."

"You won't be disappointed." The one place she and her ex had never experienced difficulty was the bedroom. Maybe that was because he'd been practicing with other women. Her rage burned with a higher flame. "Ted used to say—"

"Ted?"

She didn't want to think of him, but there he was—front and center in her mind, ruining everything. The realization stopped her short. What was she doing? Fighting her anger at Ted by making love to Nick? That was wrong, so very wrong.

This had to end. She pulled away from Nick, pivoted and ran blindly through the front room of his condo. Frantically looking for escape, she went to the sliding glass doors, threw them open and rushed outside into the moonlight. Her hands gripped the wood railing on the small balcony. Her heart thumped against her rib cage, and she was breathing hard.

The desire was still there, but she wouldn't use Nick for angry sex. He deserved better... and so did she.

He stood beside her on the balcony. The branches of a tall conifer nearly brushed the edge of the railing. The view below was landscaping that led to a manicured golf course. She stared down at the shrubs, hoping she hadn't destroyed her relationship with Nick. She liked him a lot. This was a man she could have a real relationship with.

Quietly, she said, "I'm sorry."

"I don't need an apology."

"It's just that—"

"And I don't need an explanation," he said. "All I care about is that you're safe. I'm not going to let anyone hurt you, not physically or in any other way."

She forced herself to gaze into his face. In the pale moonlight, his features were shadowed and rugged. She could tell from the way his brow pulled down that he was concerned about her. Who wouldn't be? She'd been acting like a crazy person. "This isn't me."

"Who is it?"

She was usually calm and stable. A midwife, for goodness' sake. People trusted her to deliver their babies. "Tonight was a distortion, like in a fun-house mirror."

"It's okay." His voice was gentle. "I can live with the crazy streak as long as you're honest with me."

"I swear I'll be honest."

"And I'm going to trust you, Kelly."

He smiled, and she felt acceptance. She'd behaved badly, but he wasn't kicking her to the curb. He was the kind of man who would stand by his friends. Was that what she was to him? A friend? Her relationship with Nick had the potential of being so much more than friendship.

Now wasn't the time to discuss it. "I think I need some time alone."

"Not a problem. I'll take the bedroom at the end of the hall. You take the other." He raised her hand to his lips and brushed a kiss across her knuckles. "Sleep tight."

She watched him disappear into the condo. The hand kiss was sweet and gallant, but it told her that he wanted to keep his distance, and she didn't blame him.

Her gaze lifted, and she looked up at the stars. Tears burned behind her eyelids. With all her heart, she wished that tonight had turned out differently.

*Wednesday, 9:45 a.m.*

THE NEXT MORNING after a shower, Kelly slipped into her tired khakis and shirt from yesterday and went to the front room of the condo where Nick was sitting at the dining room table.

"Good morning." He saluted her with his coffee mug. "I brewed a pot, but it's sludge. I want decent coffee from the diner in the Spencer Building."

After last night, she wasn't sure what to say. She'd already apologized, and he'd specifically told her that he didn't need for her to clarify her behavior, which was good because she wasn't sure she could tell him exactly what was going on in her head. He'd said that he wanted her to be honest. That, she could do.

She cleared her throat and said, "Going to the Spencer Building is fine with me. My van is there, and I need to pick up some fresh clothes."

"You carry a wardrobe in your van?"

"While I've been living at Serena's, I'm kind of a gypsy. Most of my stuff in Texas is in storage, but I have a couple of boxes of clothes that I'm dragging around with me."

"Ready when you are." He was already striding toward the door. "We get your clothes, then breakfast."

Before she could indulge in one more second of angst, they were on the move. Action was exactly what she needed. As they ran through simple tasks, her mind cleared and her spirit lifted. First, the van. Then, the diner. By the time she'd eaten her Denver omelet and guzzled her second cup of excellent coffee from the diner, Kelly felt as though she could take on the world.

"You stick with me today," Nick said. "If anybody starts following us, we'll take them on."

"Even if they're looking for a story about my ex?"

He leaned back in his chair and regarded her steadily. "Is there a story you want to tell them?"

She could have smeared Ted Maxwell's reputation and revealed him for the truly obnoxious jerk he was, but she preferred not to dredge up the nasty secrets of the past. "There's nothing I want to talk about."

"Honestly?"

"I don't care about my ex-husband's image. That's his problem. Honestly, I don't want to talk to the media because my past is awful, and I don't want to be hurt anymore."

"Fair enough."

His brisk tone indicated that he really didn't want to talk about this, and neither did she. "What are we going to do today?"

"I want to figure out what Uncle Samuel did with the money. His office is no longer considered a crime scene. That's where we'll start."

"I don't know how helpful I'll be." Tracking down a million dollars was way outside her experience. "I'm not good with money. I can barely balance my checkbook."

"We're not going to do accounting. I'll leave that part to Marian and Rod. We're going on a quest, and I have a feeling that you'll be good at it."

"Why?"

"You've got a talent for reading people." The waitress delivered another coffee for Nick in a to-go cup. "It always helps to have fresh eyes on a problem."

Like many creative types, he assumed that other people were as bright and clever as he was. She doubted that her fresh-eyed view would provide any new perspective, but she was willing to try. She owed him that much for putting up with her.

On the ninth floor, Nick greeted the receptionist and led Kelly down the hall to his uncle's office. The atmosphere in Spencer Enterprises had changed slightly. Kelly noticed the employees sitting up straighter and showing more respect when Nick walked by. They had to be concerned about keeping their jobs. Even in a midsize corporation like Spencer Enterprises, the death of one of the principal owners meant reorganization.

In Samuel's office, Nick sat behind the desk and pulled open the top left drawer. After emptying the back portion of the drawer of files, he reached underneath and did some kind of manipulation. The bottom of the drawer popped up.

Delighted, Kelly said, "A false bottom."

"Uncle Samuel stored his cigars in here where Julia wouldn't find them." He removed the fake panel and looked inside. "Nothing here. The forensics team from the police must have figured this out."

She leaned against the edge of the desk. "Did your uncle have a lot of these hidey-holes?"

"He liked to create illusions. Once, he told me that if he hadn't been an architect, he would have been a magician." He walked around to the front of the desk and waved an invisible wand. "Hocus-pocus, and a million dollars disappears."

"Do you think he hid the cashier's check?"

"That's too eccentric, even for Samuel. I'm looking for something that might indicate what he was doing with the money."

"Like a treasure map?"

"God, I hope not." He leaned down to inspect the molding on the front of the desk. "Somebody already opened this one, too. See how the pattern doesn't line up exactly?"

She imagined that the forensics investigating team had a ball going through this office with all the interesting little twists and turns. Samuel's cleverness extended beyond the desk. A shoe-polishing machine popped out from underneath the credenza. The wall clock twittered like a mocking bird. And a panel slid aside in the back of his closet providing a hiding place large enough for someone to hide.

The closet space worried her. "If your uncle

was killed, the murderer could have been hiding in here."

"That was one of the first things I thought of. When you were trying to revive him, I looked in here. The police dusted it for fingerprints. They found only Samuel's and mine."

"Why would he make a hiding place?"

"To get out of work." He flicked a switch and turned on a light inside the hiding space. "He used to make Julia nuts by going into his office, and then not being there when she needed him."

His uncle was beginning to sound more like a brat than a creative genius. As far as Kelly was concerned, there was a fine line between charming childlike behavior and irresponsible childishness. Samuel Spencer must have irritated a lot of people. "Any other tricks?"

"This one concerns me." He went to the window with the great view of the foothills and glided his hand under the lower sill until he found what he was looking for. "I pull the lever here, and watch."

A slot at the side of the window flipped open. The window, which hadn't appeared to be on a track, slid into it, and fresh air swept into the office.

The locked room where his uncle allegedly committed suicide hadn't been inaccessible. The open window gave an escape route for the killer.

# Chapter Eleven

*Wednesday, 11:15 a.m.*

Yesterday, Nick had shown the window trick to the police, who duly investigated and concluded that the killer hadn't lowered him or herself from the roof.

"That's not the only issue," he explained to Kelly. "The window only opens and closes from this side. If a killer used the window as an exit, it would have been open when we came through the door."

She poked her head through the window and looked down, as she'd said she wasn't afraid of heights. Then she started feeling around the edges of the window. "Maybe there's some kind of trigger on the outside."

It didn't make sense. Why would his uncle install an outdoor opener? In case a hawk wanted to swoop in for a visit? It made no sense at all, and yet...

When she pulled back inside and looked back at him, her cheeks were flushed. "I love that your uncle had a way of opening the window. One of the things I hate about offices is how you can never get fresh air."

"When this building was constructed thirty years ago, all the windows opened and closed."

"The Colorado version of air-conditioning," she said.

The climate on the front range of the Rockies was such that the temperature dropped low enough during the night to cool everything down and make air-conditioning unnecessary. At least, it used to be that way. Global warming made a difference, as did improved technology. All new construction had air-conditioning.

"The heating and cooling systems in these buildings have been updated several times. We use a lot of solar power." He remembered a discussion he'd had with Samuel about wind turbines. "My uncle was talking about tearing down the Spencer Building and starting over, creating a model for natural energy use and conservation."

"Is that a project he might borrow a million dollars to get started?"

"He might." It would be exactly like his uncle to launch into a wild-eyed project that he knew Marian and Rod and even Jared wouldn't approve of. "I was right about you bringing a new perspective. Good call, Kelly."

She did a fist pump to celebrate her insight. "Yay, me."

"If that was his plan, he must have been putting together blueprints."

"On the computer?"

"My uncle never got into computer technology."

"Really? He loved all these mechanical gizmos, but he didn't use computer science—the most fantastic gizmo of all."

"Here's how Samuel explained it to me—a magician never reveals his tricks."

She cocked her head to one side. "I don't understand."

"He liked being a genius who could dazzle his clients. It made him happy to come up with creative solutions that no one had ever considered. Computers tend to level the playing field. Anybody can sound smart if they have a free pass to the information highway. With the new architecture and blueprint software, it's a lot easier to design a building."

Nick suspected that Samuel also disdained computers because he liked to keep his secrets. If the money he'd borrowed from Radcliff had been a computer transfer, Nick could have found it in seconds. If Samuel had kept his project notes on the computer, they'd be easier to access.

"I wish I'd known him," Kelly said.

"You would have liked each other."

"Why is that?"

"You both look sweet and innocent, but you're complicated."

With the breeze through the window tossing her sunlit brown hair and a wide grin on her face, Kelly didn't appear to have a care in the world. He never would have suspected her dark side.

Last night, he'd seen into the depths of her tortured soul. She'd been hurt, and she was enraged. When she came at him, she'd been more than hot. She'd been a beast, literally tearing off his clothes. Driven by fury and passion, she'd demanded hard, rough sex. And he had been ready, so damned ready, to give it to her.

The fuse had been lit, and he knew there would be fireworks. But he'd also known that he wanted more than a down and dirty one-night stand. If he'd taken advantage of her rage at her ex-husband and indulged in angry sex, there wouldn't be a future for them. At least, that was what he'd told himself last night when he was lying alone in his bed, cursing himself for kissing her hand instead of grabbing her tight and making love to her on the balcony.

"Blueprints," she said, "aren't there like a million blueprints in the file room outside of the vault where you keep the gold?"

His brain was still fully engaged with the memory of her tongue plunging into his mouth and her fingernails clawing his back. "Blueprints?"

"For the new, improved building," she said. "Didn't you say he would have needed to draw up blueprints?"

The thought of tediously digging through the documents outside the vault gave him a headache. He reached down and manipulated the lever that closed the window. "There's something else I want to do first."

He escorted her to the elevator and they went down to the sixth floor where the sporting-goods distributor was located. This office was Nick's favorite place in the building. Nobody wore suits in these sixth- and seventh-floor offices. The employees were outdoorsy people—skiers, hikers and mountain bikers—who actually used the equipment they sold and distributed.

With the help of the receptionist, they located Tony Bracco, the chief executive, in a display area that was as big as a gymnasium. Tony was a short, lean man with a skier's tan and shaggy brown hair. In his hand, he held a crossbow.

"Hey, Nick. Sorry to hear about Uncle Sam. If there's anything I can do to help, say the word."

"How about letting me try that crossbow."

"It's a beauty."

After he introduced himself to Kelly and told her to say hi to Serena and her husband, Tony showed off the features of the crossbow, a serious weapon meant for hunting big game. "A well-aimed arrow could bring down a moose."

Nick handled the crossbow with respect, appreciating the design, the heft and the balance.

He didn't do much hunting, but when he did, he used a bow. It only seemed fair to give the prey a chance. "This baby looks more lethal than a rifle."

"You bet it is. So I guess you're not going to like it. This bow takes the challenge out of hunting."

Nick nodded to the target on the far wall. "Can I try it?"

"Knock yourself out."

He loaded the arrow, sited and fired. His arrow landed with a satisfying thump only one ring away from the bull's-eye. "Maybe I won't hunt with it, but this is fun."

Tony nudged Kelly's arm. "You want to try?"

"I'm not a shooter," she said. "I like rock climbing."

He gestured for them to come to a different area of the showroom. These offices weren't warehouses for the equipment, but they had samples of everything but guns, which were far more regulated. The latest equipment appeared first in these offices, and the sales force processed orders for shipping.

The area dedicated to mountain climbing had ropes, pitons, hinges, shoes, helmets and other goodies to make the climb safer and more efficient. Kelly picked her way through the equipment with the kind of enthusiasm that comes from awareness. She knew rock climbing.

"Do you mind if I borrow some of this stuff?" Nick asked.

"Help yourself. Going on a little outing?"

"You might say that."

With an armload of ropes, belaying equipment and grappling hooks, Nick led her back to the elevator and pressed the button for the tenth floor.

"We're going up?" She eyed him curiously. "Why?"

"Testing your theory," he said. "I want to make sure there was no way to open and close the window in Samuel's office from the outside."

On the tenth floor, he stepped into the concrete stairwell and used a piton to keep it from closing all the way. If the door locked behind them, they'd have to go all the way down to the ground floor to gain access to the building. At the door leading to the roof, it was once again necessary to prop it open and keep it from locking automatically behind them. In his office, he had keys to every door and office in the building, but there was no need to use them right now.

The view from the rooftop was panoramic, reminding him why he liked high mountains. The crisp air refreshed him, made him feel truly alive. He longed to be back home in Breckenridge, where corporate hassles were at a minimum. The small town of Valiant wasn't the place he wanted to live, not anymore. He'd rather break off his own little piece of Spencer Enterprises and leave the rest of it to his brother.

Kelly strolled across the rooftop, weaving her way between air vents and solar panels. He appreciated her long legs and athletic stride as she made her way to the side of the building facing the foothills. She leaned over the waist-high parapet.

"Your uncle's office is on this side," she said. "Is it this end or the other?"

"Right here." He dropped the equipment and studied the surroundings. "See if you notice signs that anyone else has been up here."

"Like footprints?"

"And scratches on the concrete where a hook could have been attached."

She ran her finger along the edge of the parapet. "It looks clean."

He agreed. There were no obvious physical indications that a killer had rappelled down the building, but he wasn't going to give up on the idea until he tried it himself. Precious few clues had presented themselves, and he didn't want to miss any opportunity to investigate.

Dropping to his knees, he prepared the equipment. The sadness he felt about his uncle's death was turning into something more complicated. Nick found it nearly impossible to believe that Samuel had taken his own life. He enjoyed living too much, playing games and surprising people. And the cryptic "I'm sorry" suicide note wasn't like him. Samuel had no regrets. He did what he wanted and damned the consequences. His lifestyle might drive other people—like Julia and Marian—to desperate acts, but Samuel was pretty much immune.

When he had the ropes prepared, he secured the grappling hooks with Kelly's assistance. On the off chance that he slipped, he was confident that she could use the belaying ropes to get him back up to the roof. She passed him the helmet. "Put this on."

"You're kidding, right?"

"I take safety very seriously."

He peered over the edge. "We're well over a hundred feet high. If I fall, a helmet isn't going to save me."

"Don't make me give you a lecture about how

you could lose your grip and slam into the building and knock yourself out. Or you could bump your head against a ledge. Or you—"

"Fine, I'll wear the helmet." He plunked it on his head and fastened the chinstrap. "Anything else?"

"Your shoes aren't great for climbing. The soles are too thick. And the ropes are going to ruin that nice tweed jacket. I'd give you mine, but there's no way it'd fit."

He slipped off his sports coat and adjusted the ropes. "You're kind of a pain in the rear."

"Yeah, yeah, I'm a drag." She handed him the climbing gloves. "But I've never had a serious injury while rock climbing."

Ready to make the descent, he gazed into her eyes. Standing in the morning sunlight with the wind in her hair, she was everything he wanted in a woman. Without thinking of the consequences, he leaned down and stole a quick kiss. "Wish me luck."

"Wish I was the one climbing down," she said. "Good luck."

Using the ropes, he walked backward down the building. His shoes, as Kelly had pointed out, weren't the best for traction, but he didn't slip. As he passed the window to his own office, directly above Samuel's, he peeked in. Though his office was smaller, the layout was exactly the same as Samuel's. There was a large window on this side and a smaller on the other. Instead of a square room, the office was a pentagon shape with the closet door on the corner wall at a slant facing the slanted wall with the entry door.

The wind at this height was more aggressive than on the ground. His cotton shirt was virtually no protection against the chill, but his physical exertion was enough to keep him warm. Outside his uncle's window, he inspected the bricks and ledges, looking for a device that might have been used to gain access.

Kelly called down to him. "How's it going?"

"I'm good. If I had enough rope, I'd climb all the way down to the ground."

"Finding anything?"

"No luck. I'm coming back up."

Another dead end.

WATCHING NICK CLIMB back up, Kelly felt her heart racing—not that she was worried about his safety. He knew what he was doing, and they'd set the gear to avoid mishaps. It was his casual kiss that sent her pulse into high gear.

His kiss had been natural and friendly, and she hoped with all her heart that it signaled a better direction for their relationship. She wanted to get over last night.

As she helped him over the parapet and onto the roof, she wanted another fast embrace as a reassurance that everything between them was fine. But her cell phone was ringing.

She took it out of her jacket pocket. Even though she didn't recognize the number on caller ID, she needed to answer. She was on call for several pregnant women who could go into labor at any time. She answered.

"Damn it, Kelly. What the hell is wrong with you?"

She didn't recognize the caller. "Who's this?"

"Your husband."

Her first instinct was to throw the phone off the edge of the building, but she was smarter now. She wouldn't let him hurt her. "You're my ex-husband, Ted, and I have nothing to say to you. Don't call me again."

She disconnected the call and turned back toward Nick. He'd already peeled off the helmet and was raking his fingers through his thick black hair. Looking at him, she couldn't remember what she'd ever seen in Ted, the pretty boy.

"Who was it?" Nick asked.

"The scumbag I used to be married to."

"Are you okay?"

She'd promised him honesty, and she searched her emotions for a truthful answer. "I had a flash of anger. I mean, who does he think he is? He has no right to bother me. I don't care about him anymore."

Her rage wasn't completely gone, but it was minor, no more than a hangnail. Her hands weren't shaking. Tears weren't rising up behind her eyelids. She'd gotten to a point where she simply didn't care. She was ready to forget the past. And that was the truth.

# Chapter Twelve

*Wednesday, 12:45 p.m.*

In Nick's SUV riding toward Denver, Kelly fired up her cell phone and got busy. She needed to make sure that her trip to Denver didn't cause undue problems for any of her clients. Being a midwife wasn't a regular job with regular hours. She might go days without seeing a single client, but when the call came and the client was in labor, she was there for the duration.

First, she checked in with Serena, who had already bestowed her wholehearted approval to the plan for Kelly to stay at Nick's condo. Serena reported no major problems at the Bellows farm, just the usual loveable madness with Fifi and the kids. Then, Kelly chatted with the two women who seemed most likely to go into labor within the next twenty-four hours.

She snapped her cell phone closed. "How quickly can we get back to Valiant?"

"On the highway, it'll take less than forty-five minutes," Nick said. "Are you expecting an emergency?"

"Daisy—the woman in our Lamaze class who is organic all the way—might go into labor real soon. Her water hasn't broken, but there are other symptoms."

"What happens if you're not there?"

"If the baby wants to come, that's what happens. Ready or not. If necessary, Serena can fill in for me." There was another midwife that Serena could contact if both she and Kelly were tied up, but that woman lived more than an hour away. "Let's just say that I'd like to be there for Daisy when she calls."

"We won't be in Denver for more than a couple of hours," he promised. "I'm not sure what I'll find at Radcliff's office, but I want to see the place. And I also wanted to stop by my ex-wife's house and talk to my daughters. They're kind of upset about Samuel's death."

"Is he the first of their relatives to die?"

"He's the first person they knew personally." He massaged his jaw, thinking. "This is hard. How am I going to explain to them about suicide? They're just kids."

But she knew he couldn't avoid the topic. Between the media reports and well-meaning friends, the word would certainly be spoken. "It's better if they hear about suicide from you. And also about the possibility of murder."

"I hadn't even thought about explaining a murder. These kids ask a hundred questions when a leaf falls from a branch. Why, why, why, why? I don't know what to tell them."

"A really smart guy told me to be honest," she said. "That's all you can do. You might explain what happens to a person's body when they die."

"Really?"

"I was always interested in the biology, but I suppose that's obvious since I grew up to be a nurse."

"What else? How can I talk about Samuel killing himself?"

"When you don't know the answer, that's what you say." She didn't envy him that conversation. "Where do you stand on Heaven?"

"I'm for it."

"Then that's where their great-uncle Samuel has gone."

Meeting his children also meant meeting his ex-wife. Nick hadn't said a negative word about her, and that made Kelly curious. After her experience, it was hard to imagine such a civilized end to a marriage. "You'll do fine with your kids. It sounds like you have a good relationship."

"I wish I could be with them more often.

Breckenridge is too far from Denver for them to see me every weekend, plus they have activities that keep them in town. Still, we get together at least a couple of times a month. In the summer and over Christmas vacation, they stay with me for an extended time."

A note of sadness in his voice told her that he wasn't overjoyed. "You're okay with the arrangement?"

"To be honest, I'd like to have my girls with me 24/7, but I want what's best for them. They like Denver, and their mom provides a more stable home environment than I could, because I have to take off on building projects and be on-site."

"When was the last time they saw Samuel?"

"Last Thanksgiving we had a big get-together in Valiant. Some Spencer cousins flew in from the East Coast and all of Lauren's family, even Julia's two adult children were there. Samuel took my daughters aside."

"Did he usually pay attention to the kids?"

"Not so much." The tension in his jaw relaxed as he smiled. "I remember him sitting with them in front of the fireplace and telling them stories about the heroic gold miners and the Valiant mine. He was a good storyteller. I'm glad they had that time together."

"They'll have good memories."

"I hope so."

They rode in companionable silence, watching as the skyline of downtown Denver came into sharper focus, and her mind drifted. She'd lived twelve years in the city before her divorce, and she missed the urban atmosphere. Though she liked to think of herself as someone who appreciated museums, culture and live entertainment, the truth was that she missed shopping in stores where she could find anything she wanted, from antique salt-and-pepper shakers to thermal underwear. And she missed the variety of restaurants. At the thought of food, her stomach growled.

"It hasn't been that long since breakfast," she said, "but my belly is thinking lunch."

"Radcliff's office is in lower downtown. We'll park and grab something to eat."

"Not a hot dog," she said quickly. "I can get a hot dog anywhere. There used to be a Greek place on Blake Street."

"We'll get you a pita."

They parked in a lot near Union Station and went to the corner where she'd remembered the restaurant. It had been replaced by a gourmet taco stand. She ordered two soft tacos—one with salmon, and the other with jalapeño and cream cheese. He got teriyaki beef, ground beef and a beef-and-potato combo.

They found a seat on a bench on the opposite side of the street from BR Drilling, Radcliff's local office. They'd learned that his main head-quarters were in Reno, and this storefront office sandwiched between two Realtors had a minimal crew. As she dug into her salmon taco, trying not to dribble sauce down the front of her red-and-tan jacket, she peered through the steady stream of traffic at the front window. "What are you hoping to find?"

In one bite, he consumed half of his beef-and-potato taco. "There was something that drew my uncle to this place, someone who introduced him to Radcliff. I want to get inside Samuel's head, to figure out what he was thinking."

"Why would your uncle be interested in BR Drilling?"

"They're in the business of oil leasing and development. If Samuel was doing something in the mountains, he might have crossed Radcliff's path."

"But if he was developing a project in the mountains, wouldn't he contact you?"

"You'd think so, but he liked to come up with surprises."

She wondered if Nick was hurt by not being included in his uncle's plans. In many ways, he and Samuel were similar, but Nick was more grounded in reality. He had a family and loved his kids while Samuel had never been able to settle down, not even with Julia, his long-term lover.

The sun shone full on her face as she nibbled her taco. It was a beautiful day in Denver. "I like this part of town."

"So do I. A lot of these buildings are renovations, and they've tried to keep the character of original downtown Denver." He waved his second taco toward the building crane looming over the skyline. "The city is changing. Colorado is changing."

"Growing," she said. "That's good."

"Not always. Samuel didn't think change was always good. He liked the past, the romance of the past."

After they finished their tacos, they crossed the street. In the Realtor's office next door to BR Drilling, Nick paused to study the photographs of mountain property for sale. He paid particular attention to an open field behind a barbed-wire fence with a jagged rock formation in the background.

"I know this area," he said. "It's not far from the original Valiant gold mine."

"Does your family own the land in that area?"

"We own several acres around the mine and the road leading to it. I'm not sure how much. I'd have to look it up."

She followed him into the Realtor's office, where a smiling young woman informed him that other people were interested in the property near the Valiant mine. She wouldn't give him names, but when Nick guessed Barry Radcliff, she reacted.

They didn't enter the BR Drilling offices. Nick didn't want Radcliff to know that he'd been poking around, and it was almost time to see his kids. Nick had timed his visit for the two-hour window between when his daughters got home from school and when his ex-wife's husband was off work.

They hadn't learned much by stopping at BR

Drilling, and Kelly had already figured out that the primary reason Nick had wanted to come to Denver was to see his kids and soften the blow of their great-uncle's death. She appreciated his sensitivity. A lot of people dismissed the feelings of children in a family tragedy, thinking that kids didn't need to understand death and dying. A difficult issue—she wasn't sure how she felt. The death of her child in a miscarriage had nearly destroyed her.

She braced herself to meet Nick's former wife, Wendy. Her home was a stately two-story in the Cherry Creek area. It was still too early in spring for the grass to be green, but the trees were beginning to bud and tiny shoots poked through the manicured flower beds on either side of the entrance.

Wendy opened the door for them. She was, of course, stunning. In spite of the easygoing style of her chestnut-brown hair and her casual jeans and sweater, she had an aura of polish and elegance. Kelly knew enough about clothing to recognize a designer's touch. Wendy's eyes were as blue as Nick's, but not welcoming. This was a woman who knew how to keep her distance.

She showed them into the gracious, marble-floored foyer of her home. After greeting Kelly and offering a perfunctory condolence to Nick, she said, "This situation with Samuel has gotten so ugly. A reporter contacted me for a statement."

"What did you say?"

"I referred him to my attorney. Don't worry. I won't get involved. Have the police completed their investigation?"

"Not yet." He looked toward the staircase. "Are the kids upstairs?"

"Please talk to them. I haven't known what to say."

He needed no further prompting. Nick took the stairs two at a time. A few seconds later, Kelly heard him being greeted with delighted squeals from his daughters. It was easy to imagine Nick enfolding the two girls in his arms.

"I've always thought it was important," Wendy said, "for the children to know as much as possible about their father and his family. The Spencers are an integral part of Colorado history."

Her poise was impressive. If she harbored any hostility toward Nick, she kept it well hidden. "You have a good attitude."

"I hate messy divorces, don't you?"

"You have no idea," Kelly said.

"Can I offer you a cup of coffee? Or a snack?"

"I just had lunch." And she had a dribble of taco sauce on her blouse to prove it. "But I'd love coffee, if it's no bother."

In the huge kitchen with state-of-the-art appliances, Wendy prepared two coffees using a single-cup coffeemaker. She carried the mugs to a marble-topped table in a sunlit breakfast nook. Everything about this house was organized and beautiful.

"You have a lovely home," Kelly said.

"When my husband and I bought it, the house needed a tremendous amount of renovation. Nick helped with the designs and lining up workmen. He was very useful."

And how did the new husband feel about that? It was none of Kelly's business, and she didn't ask.

"I'd hate to pry," Wendy said as she sipped her coffee, "but I simply have to ask. Are you and Nick dating?"

"I only met him a few days ago."

Kelly launched into the story about her Lamaze class and her mistaken impression that Nick and Lauren were a couple. "Lauren set me straight."

"I'll bet she did. She's a very forceful woman."

"Then Nick took me to the ninth floor to see the gold." Until this point, Kelly's narrative had been light and frothy as a cappuccino. She sounded the negative note. "That's when we found Samuel."

Apparently, Wendy was still interested because she asked about the locked room and how they tried to save the old man's life. When the story was done, she reached over and patted Kelly's hand. "Do you mind if I ask you a personal question?"

"Go right ahead."

"I heard that you're Ted Maxwell's ex-wife. What can you tell me about him?"

Instead of the usual internal explosion when she heard her ex-husband's name, Kelly felt only a twinge. She'd known that she'd have to face this question. Media people were still swarming around the investigation into Samuel's death and—like it or not—she was part of that story. The blog had upped her recognition factor by mentioning her ex, a public figure who was running for office.

"Let me put it this way," Kelly said. "I wouldn't vote for him."

Wendy did a little more prodding, but Kelly kept her lips zipped. She was beginning to get the idea that Nick's elegant ex-wife was a bit of a gossip, looking for gory details to pass on to her friends. Wendy probably ran in many of the same social circles as Ted and his new wife.

Kelly switched the subject. "I'll bet you have some stories about the Spencer family. I'm curious about Samuel. He and Julia were together for a long time. Why didn't he marry her?"

She leaned closer and lowered her voice. "There was a rumor that Julia refused to marry him unless he gave her fifty pounds of the Valiant gold. That would be a dowry of over a million dollars. Of course, Samuel refused to part with one single kilobar of the family legacy."

"That could be a symbolic gesture," Kelly said. "She might have been demanding that Samuel put her ahead of his family."

"Or it could be smart business. Julia is a shrewd woman." Wendy stood. "You might be interested in seeing a group photograph that we took last Thanksgiving when the family got together. I had it out earlier today because Maddie, my older daughter, wanted a picture of her great-uncle."

Nick and the two girls came clattering down the staircase and into the kitchen. Both children were talking at once about a goat named Fifi and a butterfly princess.

Nick explained, "I promised them a visit to Serena's farm the next time they visit Valiant." Then he introduced them to Kelly.

"I'd be happy to show you around," Kelly volunteered. "There are also a couple of llamas and bunnies and chickens."

The four-year-old clasped her hands together and whispered, "I love bunny rabbits."

The seven-year-old girl was more serious. Her eyes were red as though she might have been crying. She tugged on her father's arm. "Come and see the picture."

"It's in the dining room on the table," Wendy said. "I need to have it framed."

In the dining room, Kelly looked around Nick's shoulder as Maddie carefully spread the eight-by-fifteen-size photo on the table. There must have been thirty people in the group—all ages, sizes and shapes. Maddie tried to put names with all the faces, and Nick helped biographical details.

"That's a cousin from New York, a doctor. That dude with the beard does shipwreck salvage in Florida."

"What's salvage?" Maddie asked.

"Your mom can explain."

"No, she can't," Wendy said. "You're going to have to write this down, Nick. I can't remember all these people."

"Here's the important one," Nick said as he pointed to a white-haired gentleman in a suit. "Your great-uncle Samuel."

Maddie kissed the tip of her finger and touched it to Samuel's chest. The simple, sweet gesture stirred Kelly's heart. She wanted to hug this little girl and promise her that everything would be all right.

Before she lifted her gaze from the photograph, Kelly glimpsed a face that she'd seen before. His eyes stared directly at her, and he seemed to be laughing. "Who's this?"

"Julia's son, Arthur Starkey."

Arthur Starkey was the man who had been tailing her in Valiant.

# Chapter Thirteen

*Wednesday, 6:15 p.m.*

"I believe you." Nick drove into the cul-de-sac in Valiant where his sister-in-law's house took up two and a half lots on the back end. "But I still don't like it."

"Fine," Kelly said. "Next time I recognize a bad guy, I'll try to make it someone you don't care about."

"I'm not buddy-buddy with Arthur. I've told you that. Hell, I don't even like the guy."

"But you care about Julia."

Though dusk had barely settled, every light in the Spencer house seemed to be lit. A couple of days ago, Lauren had been complaining about not having anyone around; now it appeared that a mob of friends and family had arrived to offer help and condolence. Several vehicles blocked the circular drive outside the front entrance. Near the three-car garage, he recognized Julia's bronze Lexus.

Nick parked his SUV at the curb. He turned off the engine but made no move to get out of the car. "It all comes down to the same thing. Somehow, I'm going to have to tell Julia that her son might be involved in Samuel's death."

"We don't know he's involved," Kelly said.

On the drive from Denver, they had gone around and around, trying to come up with reasons why Arthur might have been lurking around in Valiant and following Kelly. Was he working with Trask? Had he hired the private investigator? Did he want to talk to Kelly about Samuel's dying words? Was there some other connection? Too many questions, not enough answers.

"I need to talk to Arthur." But the phone number Nick had was disconnected. "I might be able to avoid a conversation with Julia if I just ask for his phone number."

Kelly reached over and touched his arm. "She'll ask you why you need to talk to her son, and you'll have to say something. Julia is sharp. You won't be able to hide anything from her."

He could tell that she wanted him to lean on her. She was so slim and delicate that he kept forgetting that she was also strong. "I'm glad you're with me. It would have been worse to make these decisions by myself."

"I want to help. I'll do anything I can."

Later tonight, when they were alone at his condo, he had a pretty good idea of how he'd like to take her up on that offer. But that didn't help with the current problem. He looked toward the sprawling house. "It's possible that Arthur is inside, mingling with everybody else and acting like he belongs."

"There's another way to handle this," she

said. "Contact the police and let them question Arthur."

He shook his head. "I'm not going to get Julia's son in trouble unless I'm sure he deserves it."

"Do you want me to talk to Julia?"

A tempting offer, but he couldn't push this confrontation off on her. "I've got to do it myself."

He shoved open his door and came around the SUV to the curbside where she was standing and waiting. Her eager, tenuous smile encouraged him and told him that she cared, really cared, about what happened to him. When she reached out and took his hand, he wanted a deeper connection.

His arm slipped around her waist, and he reeled her in, gradually pulling her closer until her body pressed against his.

"What do you think you're doing?" she asked in a teasing whisper.

"Looking for inspiration."

"Take whatever you want."

Her lips parted, inviting him. When they kissed, he felt a rush, like adrenaline pounding through his veins, urging him to go faster and harder. He wanted to make love to her. Later tonight, he promised himself. If she was ready, so was he.

At the front door, Nick walked inside without ringing the bell. The house used to belong to his parents, and Nick grew up here which gave him a certain feeling of ownership. The colors and furniture were different, but the atmosphere was the same. He could see where the stained glass in the window by the door had been repaired after he'd knocked a home run through it. The wall beside the staircase was lined with photos of Spencer ancestors that had been there for as long as Nick could recall.

Avoiding other conversations, he made his way down the hall to the kitchen where dinner was being prepared. Lauren grabbed Kelly and gave her a knife to cut salad veggies, leaving him alone to find Julia. She was in the dining room, setting the table.

When he entered, she looked up. "Shall I set another two places for you and Kelly?"

"We're not staying," he said.

"I'm glad you suggested that I come over here. Living alone, I forget how nice it is to have a family. So many people have told me their fond memories of dear Samuel."

That might have been the first time he'd ever heard her refer to his uncle as *dear.* Their relationship was feisty, not sentimental, and he wasn't buying the image of Julia as a pathetic figure. He'd witnessed some world-class arguments between her and Samuel. She was tough as steel.

"We need to talk," he said. "Out here on the porch, we can grab a little privacy."

"Could be chilly." She adjusted the collar on her black turtleneck and pulled her gray cardigan more tightly around her. "But I have my sweater, so I ought to be warm enough."

He opened the French doors and led her into an enclosed porch that was a favorite spot for breakfast on summer days. Unheated, it was cooler than the family dining room but not freezing. The air smelled stale, as though memories of better times had come here to die and had rotted.

This conversation with Julia would forever change his relationship with her. He was accusing her son. Nick would no longer be the young man she cared for like a nephew. He would be her adversary.

After he turned on the overhead light, he plunged right in. "I need to find Arthur. Do you know how I can reach him?"

"What's he done now?"

"I just want to talk to him."

"Because you're such great friends?" Her sarcasm was biting and more in character with Julia's personality than her show of wistful sentiment. "You and Arthur were raised as close as brothers but never warmed up to each other. Tell me why you're after my son."

The way she phrased her statement made Arthur sound like a victim, which he sure as hell was not. Julia's son was in his forties, older than Nick or Jared, and he'd never done an honest day's work. There was always some scheme Arthur was running, a big payoff that was right around the corner.

Nick lowered himself into one of the chairs at the glass-topped breakfast table. "Something is going on with Arthur. What do you know about it?"

Anger narrowed her gaze. For a moment he thought she was going to turn on her heel and storm away from him. "I don't know what you're talking about."

"Don't play games with me."

"I've never seen this side of you, Nick. You sound just like your uncle."

He wouldn't let her cajole him into dropping his questions. It was time to pull out the big guns. "I have evidence that Arthur is involved with some bad people. Don't make me take it to the police."

"Fine." She pulled out another chair from the table and sat. "For the very first time in both their lives, Samuel and Arthur were working together. Frankly, I was pleased. It was always my dream for Samuel to love my children and think of them as his own. I should have known there'd be trouble."

Finally Nick felt as if he was making progress. "What were they working on?"

"I don't know the details," she said. "I purposely kept my distance so the two of them would have more time together, and Samuel could see that Arthur really does have good ideas, especially when it comes to creative financing."

"The kind of financing that Barry Radcliff does?"

"That's correct." Her long fingers knotted

into fists. "Arthur arranged the first meeting between Samuel and Mr. Radcliff."

That puzzle was solved, and it made perfect sense. A con man like Arthur would have contacts that weren't 100 percent legit, and Samuel would enjoy the thrill of getting money without consulting Marian or Rod or even Julia.

"Do you remember when I told you that Samuel put up the Valiant gold as collateral for the loan?"

"I most certainly do," Julia snapped. An angry flush colored her cheeks. "A foolish mistake."

"If I don't pay Radcliff, he might find a way to take his payment in kilobars."

"That's absurd, Nick. I won't let that happen."

It might not be her decision. "That's why I need your help. I've got to have more information. Tell me what Samuel was working on."

"I don't know."

He didn't believe her. "Sooner or later, I'll find out. A million dollars doesn't just vanish into thin air. There have to be records."

"You're so naive, Nick. Your uncle never wrote anything down. He never filed anything. No one at Spencer Enterprises would have known what he was doing if it wasn't for me."

"You and Samuel together made the perfect partnership." He was creative, and she was organized. "He trusted you."

"Barely noticed me," she said. "Half the time I was invisible to him."

"You've got to tell me everything. I don't want to lose the gold."

Still putting up a fight, she looked down at her clenched fingers. "The more I think about it, the more I'm sure it has something to do with the Valiant gold mine in the mountains. Remember, I told you that I saw a credit-card charge from the Hearthstone Motel."

"How do I find Arthur?"

She recited a phone number. "It's a cell phone, and he hasn't been answering for the past few days."

"Home address?"

"I can't help you with that," she said. "You know how Arthur is. He doesn't like to put down roots. For the past six months he hasn't had a permanent address. He stays with friends. Most of his belongings are stored at my place."

"If he contacts you, will you let me know?"

"I can't promise that," she said.

Nick looked her in the eye, searching for a glimmer of their former friendship. He hated to lose his connection with her; Julia was a link to his uncle. As she gazed back at him, he didn't see a welcome sign. "I'll keep you informed."

"Don't hurt him." Her voice dropped to a lower register. "Please, Nick. Don't hurt my son."

That wasn't his plan. Nick wanted only one thing: to understand how and why his uncle had died. The million dollars and the Valiant kilobars of gold were secondary. If the money was lost, so be it. He couldn't lose Samuel without knowing the truth.

THOUGH LAUREN DID HER BEST to make him stay, Nick pleaded exhaustion and made his escape with Kelly. He sure as hell didn't want to sit down to dinner with Julia glaring at him. A couple of the other women were interested in his relationship with Kelly. The more serious-minded wanted to talk about Samuel and the plans for the memorial service.

He dived behind the steering wheel of his SUV and allowed the cool, dark silence to enfold him. Kelly sat beside him, not speaking. During their time together, they'd developed an ability to read each other's rhythms. He didn't have to tell her that he needed quiet—she just knew.

When he reached blindly toward her, she stuck a home-baked chocolate-chip cookie in his hand. He hadn't known that he was hungry until he chomped down on the cookie.

"Perfect," he said with a satisfied moan.

"While I was in the kitchen," she said, "I

threw together a couple sandwiches and grabbed cookies. There's also fruit."

"I'll take another cookie."

"Thought so. You've been running around and stressing out all day. It's important to keep your energy level in balance."

"Is that expert nutritional advice?"

"Common sense," she said. "And I couldn't help noticing that you don't have any food at your condo."

"I've got coffee."

"And beer and half a carton of questionable eggs that might have been there for months. Typical bachelor's pad."

Her description wasn't really fair. Because he didn't spend much time at the Valiant condo, he didn't bother stocking it with supplies. "My house in Breckenridge has plenty of healthy stuff."

"But we're not there, are we?"

He wished they were. He would have been happy to erase these few days and start over.

"It would have been nice to meet you in a more normal way."

"Maybe." She handed him a fat roast-beef sandwich and some paper towels.

"Explain."

"If you and I had bumped into each other on the street in Breckenridge and started dating, it would have taken weeks, maybe months, for me to get this close. I would have been cautious because of my lousy first marriage, and I certainly wouldn't have had the kind of meltdown I had last night."

"And that's a good thing?" He bit into the roast beef, an excellent sandwich.

"I probably wouldn't recommend starting off a relationship with a nervous breakdown, but it certainly cuts through a lot of protective shields. It takes a lot to make me angry, and last night I was an erupting volcano."

And hotter than any woman he'd ever known. "Some parts of that, I liked."

"I know." She nibbled at her own sandwich.

"Before we go back to your place, should we stop at the supermarket?"

"There's something else I want to do first."

"What did Julia tell you?" She handed him a bottled water.

He unscrewed the cap and took a drink. "How did you get out of the house with all this stuff."

"Big purse," she said. "Julia?"

Between bites he told her about Arthur introducing Samuel and Radcliff and about the project near the gold mine that they were supposedly working on together. "Supposedly, Arthur doesn't have an address or a phone that he answers, but Julia said that her son stores a lot of his stuff at her house."

"Are you suggesting that we break in to her house?"

"I helped build the place. I know my way around the alarm system."

"Couldn't we tell Julia what we're doing and ask her for a key?"

"Right now, she's not in a mood to cooperate with me."

He finished off his sandwich and started the engine. Looking for clues in Arthur's stuff was progress. Nick had a really good feeling about this break-in.

# Chapter Fourteen

*Wednesday, 8:32 p.m.*

Kelly had a really bad feeling about this break-in. From the first time she met Julia, she'd sensed that Uncle Samuel's longtime secretary and lover was a woman with a lot of secrets. The biggest mystery was why she and Samuel never married. Something kept Julia from saying "I do."

Though it was possible that Samuel had never asked her to get hitched, Kelly found that doubtful. The man had built a magnificent house just for her. The details he incorporated in the design, like the three-story library and the shimmering stained glass, showed that he knew her well and took her interests seriously. Of course he'd asked.

Why would she say no? Maybe she didn't think Samuel would be a good stepfather. From what Nick told her, Julia was protective of her children. That had to be difficult with a problem kid like Arthur. What about Julia's daughter? Nobody talked much about her.

Kelly glanced over at Nick. The mountain road leading to Julia's house was extremely dark—the only illumination came from the dashboard lights. He looked mysterious…and determined.

She asked, "Is Julia's daughter coming to Valiant for the memorial service?"

"She might. She and my uncle seemed to get along fairly well, and they had interests in common."

"Is she an architect?"

"More of an artist. Annette works for one of the top clothing designers in New York, and

I've heard that she might be starting her own line of shoes and handbags."

"Married?"

"For twelve years. No kids, though. The last time I saw her, she was carrying around a yappy little dog with a rhinestone collar."

"And what does she think of her brother?"

"Arthur has pretty much burned his bridges with everybody in the family. Annette told me that he came to visit her in New York and seriously overstayed his welcome. She was ticked off about a loan she made to him that wasn't ever going to get repaid."

When they rounded the last curve leading to Julia's house, Kelly saw lights through the canted front windows and from farther back in the house. "Someone's here."

"It's got to be Arthur." Nick sounded excited. "I should have figured this out. I knew he was here in Valiant following you, which means he needed a place to stay. Why not here with mom?"

Though Kelly wasn't an aggressive person, she wished they had some kind of weapon to protect themselves. Arthur might be dangerous. "If we keep after bad guys, you might want to rethink your no-guns policy."

"Arthur won't hurt us. He's a con man, not a hit man."

She wasn't so sure. Arthur had been following her, stalking her through the streets. When Nick parked the SUV in the driveway, she said, "You're not making any attempt to be secretive. I guess that means we're not breaking in."

"Not when I can walk up to the door and ring the bell." He looked toward her. "Are you scared?"

"A little," she admitted. "I don't know Arthur like you do, but he sounds like a desperate person. He was tailing my car, watching me on the street. I don't know what he was after, and I don't think I want to find out."

He reached toward her and gently stroked the

line of her jaw. "You can stay in the car with the motor running and the doors locked."

Hiding in the car while she knew Nick was in peril frightened her more than facing her stalker. "What if he's not alone? What if he's got a hit man in there with him?"

"Stay here. If I don't signal you in ten minutes, call 911."

They were in the middle of nowhere. It would take the police forever to respond. She peered through the windshield at the house, and her imagination ran wild, seeing an army of thugs lurking in the shadows. She definitely didn't want to be alone with her fear. "I'll come with you."

She followed him up the winding path that led to the stained-glass mosaic above the front entryway. Wind rustled through the branches of the pines and conifers at the edge of the house. She heard rippling water from the fountain in the Japanese garden. The atmosphere had been designed for serenity, but her heart was pounding like a jackhammer. She stayed a step behind Nick with her weight on her back foot, ready to run at the slightest hint of threat.

The doorbell resonated with rich alto tones. Though she couldn't identify the noises she heard from inside, somebody was moving around. "He's not exactly rushing to the door," she said.

Nick pushed the doorbell again and called out, "Arthur, it's me, Nick Spencer. I want to talk to you."

To her right, she heard the click of a door closing. Nick stepped off the porch to look in that direction. He swore under his breath. "He's running."

She wouldn't have minded letting Arthur get away. As far as she was concerned, he was acting like a guilty man who should be turned over to the authorities. But Nick had already taken off in pursuit. She had no choice but to follow.

Nick ran along the edge of the house toward the deck. With his long-legged stride, he pulled away from her quickly. Kelly slung her purse strap across her chest and concentrated on moving fast. Following him, she descended a slope at the edge of the deck and darted into the surrounding forest.

Her years of rock climbing made her surefooted, but it was dark and she wasn't familiar with the terrain. She had to slow down so she wouldn't twist an ankle.

Nick kept moving, dodging through the trees and leaping over rocks in his path. He was a powerful runner. There was no way she could keep up with him, and they were moving farther away from the house and the car.

Nick was still headed downhill when she caught sight of a man hiding in the shadows by a stand of aspen. Nick had gone too far. She was closer to the man.

"This way," she yelled. Her breath was nearly gone. "Nick, come back this way."

The man turned toward her. He was too far away for her to see his face, but she felt his gaze boring into her. He peeled away from the trees and came at her. Where was Nick? Hadn't he heard her calling him?

If she went in the direction she'd seen Nick running, she'd crash right into the man. Making a pivot, she headed toward where she thought the road should be. Dry brush and pine needles crunched under her feet. She ducked to avoid the low-hanging limbs of pine trees and dodged around thick shrubs.

She stumbled and went down on her hands and knees. He was getting close. She could hear him. "Nick, over here. He's over here."

There was no way she could outrun this guy in the forest where every rock was trying to trip her. If she made it to the road where the footing was better, she might have a chance in a full-out sprint. She looked over her shoulder. He was tall, not muscular like Nick, but tall.

He called to her. "Kelly, that's your name, right? Kelly, wait up."

She had to make a stand. Coming to a dead

stop, she yanked her purse off her shoulder. Slinging it by the strap, she could use it as a weapon. "Stay away from me."

Ten feet from her, he stopped. In the moonlight she could make out his features. He was the same person who had been following her in Valiant—Arthur Starkey.

"I mean it," she yelled, swinging her purse in a wide arc. "Don't come any closer."

"I'm not going to hurt you."

"Damn right you're not." She swung her purse again, and he stepped back. "Why were you following me? What do you want?"

"Just calm down." He held up both hands in an appeasing gesture. "It's all good. Nothing to worry about."

Nick dived through the trees and tackled Arthur. They were both down on the ground. It took less than a minute for Nick to flip him onto his belly and jam his knee in the center of Arthur's back, pinning him to the ground.

He looked up at her. "Are you all right?"

"I think so." She was shaken. Her heart was still racing, and she was sweating hard.

"You're sure? No bumps? No bruises?"

"I'm fine."

On the ground, Arthur squirmed. "Get off me."

"Not until you tell me why you ran."

"I wasn't sure it was you at the door. There are people who want to kill me."

"Like who?"

Arthur continued to struggle, trying to get up. "There's this guy named Trask."

"Liar!" Kelly flung her purse on the ground and bent to stare into his face. "I saw you in the car with Trask."

"That's right. I was following you, and then this white-haired guy appears out of nowhere and gets in my car. He tells me to back off. He says I'd better get out of town."

She didn't know if she could believe him. Arthur had a reputation for being a liar and a scam artist. "Why were you following me in the first place?"

"I heard you were with Samuel when he died."

"What does that mean to you?" Nick demanded. "Why do you care?"

"You're not the only one who lost someone important to them. Samuel was like a father to me." The pitch of Arthur's voice was smooth, too smooth to be believed. "I want to find out who killed him."

Nick lifted his knee from Arthur's back and rose to his feet. When Arthur scrambled up, the two men stood facing each other, each taking the measure of the other. Nick was clearly in better shape than Arthur, who was too skinny, with hunched shoulders. He was older than Nick, and the years had taken a toll. His narrow face was lined, and his nose was crooked as though it had been broken and improperly set. His thin mouth and dark eyes showed a resemblance to his mother.

Nick spoke first. "You think Samuel was murdered."

"Don't you? He wasn't the kind of guy who commits suicide, especially not now. He had everything to live for."

"Julia told me you were working with him."

"Maybe I was," Arthur said, "and maybe I just told my mother that to keep her off my back. She always said she liked it when me and Samuel spent time together, but when it got right down to it, she wanted him all to herself."

Kelly remembered the story Nick's ex-wife had told her about Julia refusing to marry Samuel unless he parted with the family gold. Arthur might have a valid point about her jealousy. At the same time, she reminded herself that Arthur Starkey couldn't be trusted. It was a typical con man trick to lay down a thread of truth before spinning a web of lies.

"Why were you stalking me?" she asked. "If you had questions, you could have introduced yourself like a normal person and asked me."

"Like a normal person," he said with a cold smile. "Is that why you're dating good old Nicky? You like things to be normal?"

"Knock it off," Nick said.

"You're Mr. Normal, you know you are. Nicky Spencer is the guy everybody likes, the guy you can count on to do the right thing. Not a superstar like your brother. That bothered your pretty little wife, didn't it? She wanted the boss, not the back-up quarterback."

Nick didn't rise to the bait. "Kelly asked you a question. Why the stalking?"

"Are you going to stand there like a big dumb ox and let me insult you? In front of your new girlfriend?"

"I don't have time for your games, Arthur."

"What are you going to do? Knock me down again?"

A muscle in Nick's jaw twitched. Otherwise he was cool. The childish taunts had to be irritating, and she admired Nick for ignoring them.

Quietly he said, "Believe me, Arthur, I don't

like asking you for help. I'd rather consult with a homicidal Colombian drug lord than to make you my ally. But the truth is that we both want the same thing—to find Samuel's killer. If you ever cared at all for my uncle, you'll talk to me."

Arthur ran his hand along his jaw, wiping off his sneer. "I wasn't stalking Kelly. My plan was to approach her, but Trask scared me off before I could make my move."

"What did you want to ask her?"

Arthur turned to her. "I thought Samuel might have said something before he died that would identify his killer."

"He wasn't coherent," Kelly said, "and I was too busy trying to stop the bleeding to listen carefully. He told me to close the door."

"Which door?" Arthur asked.

"There was only one door to the room. It had to be that one."

"And the closet," Nick said. "There was also the closet door. Don't worry, Arthur, I checked in Samuel's hideout to make sure nobody was in there."

Arthur turned back to her. "Anything else?"

"Something about gold. He repeated the word several times. And he talked about a heart of stone."

"Heart of stone," Arthur repeated. "I was hoping for something more. Let's head back to the house."

Instead of hiking up the slope they'd raced down, Nick and Arthur went to the right. The two-lane road was only twenty yards away. They walked abreast with Nick in the middle. After dodging down the hill in the dark, the asphalt under her feet felt as smooth as marble.

"You introduced Samuel to Radcliff," Nick said.

"I made that connection. Samuel needed to borrow money from an untraceable source, and I was happy to help out. Samuel paid me four thou as a finder's fee. It should have been more."

"And you don't know what he did with the money. Or what he intended to do."

"I can tell you this much," Arthur said. "It had something to do with the Valiant gold mine. If I had to guess, I'd say he was looking into starting up the mining operations again."

Nick scoffed. "That's pretty far-fetched."

"Is it? Oil might be king, but gold keeps going up in value. A gold mine would be a hell of a lot more profitable than the current housing market."

"Why keep it a secret?"

"You know how Samuel was. He liked to play tricks like a magician. He could pull a solid-gold rabbit out of his hat and save the precious family business."

Kelly thought Arthur's ideas fit with what she knew of Samuel's character. He liked to do the unexpected, like setting an office park with a ten-story building in a low-population town like Valiant. "If he opened the mine again, would that be a motive to kill him?"

"It's a risky venture," Nick conceded.

"And there are people who want to control Spencer Enterprises," Arthur said. "I'm thinking of Marian Whitman and Rod Esterhauser. They want to steer the ship. The two of them are as cutthroat and greedy as a couple of pirates."

Greedy enough to commit murder? Kelly shuddered.

# Chapter Fifteen

*Wednesday, 9:24 p.m.*

Nick wished he could dismiss Arthur's accusations, but the little weasel had hit on a theory that had been playing around in the back of Nick's mind. He had been considering Marian as a suspect—not because of nefarious motives to take control of the business but because she was the only other person nearby when Samuel was shot. She might have staged the moment when they had to break down the door.

"You know I'm right," Arthur said. "The killer is one of those upstanding citizens, maybe both of them. They did it. They're scum. And they have to pay."

"If they're guilty."

"Take off the blinders, Nicky. These people are nicey-nice with you, but I know them from a different perspective. I can't count the number of doors they've slammed in my face."

Nick didn't want to waste time raking over the coals of old grudges. Marian had pulled the plug on a couple of Arthur's investment schemes. So what? Nick had also turned him down. His own sister wouldn't loan him money.

"I get it," he said. "You don't like lawyers and accountants. But that's not proof. You still haven't explained what Marian or Rod stand to gain by killing Samuel."

"They'd get their dirty little paws on Samuel's stock. He owned 33 percent of Spencer Enterprises."

"How do you know that figure?" Nick asked.

"It's my inheritance."

Arthur's murky logic was beginning to come

clear. Nick hadn't known he was the beneficiary. "You inherit, and the company has to pay you for the value of the stock."

"And I become a wealthy man." He chuckled to himself. "Then Rod and Marian buy my shares or shuffle it into the corporate pool that they manage. Either way, they get controlling interest."

"Not entirely," Nick said. "Jared and I still own 40 percent."

"And Samuel always voted with you. With him out of the way, the Spencer magic is over. Marian and Rod can take over."

*An ugly scenario.* Though Nick didn't like the constrictions of corporate business, he wasn't willing to throw away his birthright. If bean counters like Marian and Rod were running the show, Spencer Enterprises would be only about the bottom line. Property holdings would be sold or leased, building projects would be outsourced, and there would be no new architecture, no creativity.

"I have a question," Kelly piped up. "How do you know that Samuel made you his beneficiary?"

"You're cute and smart," Arthur said. "An impressive combo. I like her, Nicky."

"Answer her question."

"Your uncle loved my mother. That's no big secret. Everybody knew it. He liked to give her presents, but Mom didn't care for jewelry or fancy vacations. She's a practical woman." He gestured to the beautifully designed structure they were approaching. "She asked Samuel for a house, and he delivered. She asked for financial security for herself and her kids. Samuel wrote us into his will. He told me. My sister gets property. I get stock."

"Have you seen the will?" Nick asked.

"No." He paused in the middle of the road to take a breath. "I know what was promised to me. That's why I'm hanging around here. I need final confirmation."

That was the truest statement Arthur had

made. He was hovering like a vulture, waiting to hear the reading of Samuel's will.

"That's interesting," Nick said. "I thought you were here because you were investigating my uncle's death. Seeking justice for his murder. Punishing the wrongdoers."

Arthur clapped him on the shoulder. "Now that I know you're on the case, I'll step back. You can handle it."

"Give me a phone number where I can reach you."

"Why should I?" Arthur turned his back and walked toward the driveway where Nick's SUV was parked.

"You need me," Nick said.

"Why?"

"Because I'm an insider and you aren't. I can find out the actual terms of Samuel's will. I could find out tomorrow. As soon as I have information, I'll let you know."

Arthur gave an unpleasant little chuckle.

"Who would have ever thought you and I would be working together?"

Since he didn't have a card with his current number, they waited while Kelly dug through her purse and found a scrap of paper and a pen. Nick made a note of the number, which would come in handy if he needed to contact Arthur again.

"Are you going to be staying at the house?" Nick asked.

"Might as well. Mom is off playing Lady Bountiful at Lauren's place. It could be her last chance to reap the benefits of being Samuel's longtime companion. With your uncle out of the picture, nobody is going to pay much attention to her."

"I would," Nick said.

"Yeah, sure. After your kids and your brother and whatever chick you're dating, you might get around to saying hello to Julia and reminiscing about the good old days when you and me helped your uncle build this house."

A thought occurred to Nick. "You knew it was me as soon as I rang the doorbell."

"How do you figure?"

"You went out the side door onto the deck. If it had been anybody else you would have taken the secret passageway and hidden in the basement. You and I are the only ones who know about the sliding door in the bedroom and the staircase."

"And I would have been trapped in the basement. Good call, Nicky."

"Why did you run?" Nick asked.

"Haven't you figured it out yet?" Arthur spread his arms wide. "I don't like you. Not you or your brother or any of the other Spencer family trust funders. When I have my money, I promise that you Spencers will never see me again."

He swept low in a bow, pivoted and jogged up the stair to the house that Samuel built. It was a ridiculous and dramatic exit, appropriate for a ridiculous man. Nick would be happy for the day when Arthur was out of his life for good.

In a quiet voice, Kelly asked, "How much of that do you think we can believe?"

"He's not to be trusted, that's for sure." He wrapped his arm around her and pulled her close. "I thought you saw the good in everyone."

"It's hard to be positive about somebody who chases you through the forest. Arthur scared me half to death."

"But you fought him off with your purse." He kissed the top of her head. "I don't think he's a real threat, but I'm not sure. Arthur is desperate. When he knew it was me at the door, he took off running."

"You've known him since you were kids," she said. "Has he done that before?"

As a general rule, Arthur stood his ground and defended himself with a wall of insults. But he'd been afraid to face Nick. "He's got something to hide. We can believe some of what he said to us, but he's leaving a lot out."

She tilted her face toward him. "I almost feel sorry for him. He was raised with all you Spencers but never really felt like part of the family."

"That was his choice."

As he gazed down at her, other thoughts fled from his mind. The rest of the night belonged to them. Taking her arm, he directed her to the passenger side of his SUV. If he drove fast, his condo was only twenty-five minutes away from here, and it was going to be hard to wait that long before he started kissing her.

"Arthur was an outsider." She came to a stop at the car door. "Believe me, I know what that's like. It can warp a person."

"Can we stop talking about Arthur?" He yanked open the door. When she climbed inside, he ran around to the driver's side and got behind the steering wheel. In seconds, he had his seat belt on, had the engine started and was backing into the road.

"When I was with my ex," she said, "his job required us to go to lots of gala events. I always felt like an oddball. I didn't know the people in that crowd, and there wasn't a reason for them to pay attention to me. I wasn't famous or stunningly beautiful or powerful. So, I got ignored. I spent a lot of time alone in a corner with the potted plants."

"That was your ex-husband's fault. He should have made sure you were comfortable with the people around you." Every time she talked about that jerk, Nick had another reason to hate Ted Maxwell. "Any man who escorted you would be the luckiest man in the room."

"Thank you, but you're just being nice."

"I've watched you in action, and your behavior is always appropriate, whether you're pretending to be a dragon or meeting a top executive. People like you. They like to talk to you. Kelly, you made a friend of my ex-wife, and that's not easy."

"You might be prejudiced in my favor." But he heard in her voice that she was pleased. If he could have seen her in the dark, he suspected she'd be smiling. "I was using my experience to show you how it feels to be an outcast, like Arthur."

"You're nothing like him. Even when he was a kid, Arthur was working the angles, trying to get something for nothing."

"As a desperate plea for attention?"

"He was treated fairly," Nick said. There were a lot of things wrong with his family, but this wasn't one of them. "The Spencers have money and a certain amount of status, but we're open-minded. That's a tradition in the West."

"How so?"

"You can't be a rancher or a gold miner all by yourself. You need other people doing their jobs and doing them right. It's something you learn when you work together, especially when you live close to nature. In a blizzard or a forest fire, everybody pitches in. Everybody is valued."

"I never thought of it that way."

"If you pull your own weight, we're glad to have your help, and you're rewarded. The first time you saw me in my tuxedo, I'd been at a ceremony giving scholarship awards to deserving teenagers. That's my family's legacy."

Pride surged through him. He hadn't realized that he felt so deeply about this topic. "Arthur went out of his way to spit on our heritage. He bitched and whined and claimed that he deserved more. Something for nothing, that was his motto. It still is, and I don't feel the least bit sorry for him."

"You have strong feelings about this."

"Damn right, I do." He cranked the steering wheel to make a sharp turn on the twisting mountain road. "It might seem silly to hang on to the antique mining tools and the paintings and the kilobars of Valiant gold, but that's who I am. It's who Samuel was."

"Okay," she said, "forget about Arthur's personality and think about what he said. He's certain that Samuel was murdered."

"Even a broken clock is right twice a day."

Arthur had been right about a couple of

things. Rod and Marian were ambitious and wanted more control of the business, and they had been putting pressure on his uncle to retire. Still, murdering Samuel to get his 33 percent of the company stock seemed like a roundabout way of taking over, not to mention the negative light it shone on Spencer Enterprises."

"He mentioned the gold mine," Kelly said.

"That's where I think Arthur was holding back. He knows more about Samuel's project than he was telling us."

He guided the SUV off the winding road onto a more main thoroughfare. Only ten minutes away from his condo, his anticipation was building. Stopping to pick up groceries might be smart, but his hunger had nothing to do with food.

"We're almost to your place," she said.

"Are you tired?"

"Kind of."

"If you'd want, I could give you a nice, long massage."

"I'd like that."

Her voice held a slightly husky tone, and he hoped he wasn't imagining her interest. Agreeing to a massage was a step in the right direction; it meant she wanted him to touch her.

Realizing that he was speeding twenty miles over the limit, he eased up on the accelerator. "We could have some wine, just lie back and relax."

"That's a good place to start."

Where did a nontherapeutic massage lead except to bed? There was no mistaking her intention. He wouldn't be sleeping alone tonight. And then he heard the ring for her cell phone.

She answered right away.

Nick was praying that it wasn't anything important, but he heard her ask how far apart the contractions were and he heard her promise to be there as soon as she could.

Kelly ended the call and sank back against the passenger seat. "That was Daisy. Her water broke an hour ago, and she's going into labor."

"What do you want to do?"

"I want to go home with you," she said. "I want that wine and the massage."

*Don't toy with me, woman.* He wanted that, too. "And?"

"I've got to be with Daisy. This is her first baby. Even though she's studied the natural and organic ways to give birth, she needs me." She exhaled a deep sigh. "We need to stop by the Spencer Building so I can pick up my van."

Reluctantly, he adjusted his course. They wouldn't make love tonight…not unless Daisy went through labor and delivery in record speed. "My ex-wife was in labor for twelve hours with Maddie."

"Not unusual," she said.

Nick just couldn't catch a break. "There's something else to consider. One of the reasons I want to keep you with me is for your own protection. We still don't know what's going on with Trask. If Arthur is to be believed, he might be more dangerous than we first suspected."

"I can't have you hanging around while Daisy is in labor. She needs to be calm and serene. I can call you if I see Trask."

"Which would be too late," he said. "It's better if I wait outside on the street and keep an eye on the house."

"All night?" She reached toward him. Her touch on his arm reminded him of what he was going to be missing. "How are you going to investigate if you're spending the night in your SUV?"

There was another solution—one he hadn't used because he wanted the job as Kelly's protector for himself. "I'll contact O'Shea and arrange security. They'll be instructed to be subtle and not disturb Daisy's house. You'll never know they're there, but they'll be ready if you need them."

"I've never had a bodyguard before."

"You'll like these guys. They have guns."

He dropped her off at her van. In his vehicle, he followed her to Daisy's house, parked at the curb and got out. He wanted to prolong his time with her, even if it meant nothing more than walking her to the door.

From the back of her van, Kelly took her regular satchel, her purse and another backpack. Apparently, she was moving in with Daisy for the duration of labor.

"That's a lot of equipment." He picked up the backpack to help. "Are you delivering a baby or building a small city?"

"Architecture is your game," she said. "I don't build, I facilitate. But you'd be amazed by how much of this stuff actually comes in handy."

She hopped down from the van and slid the door closed. Before she picked up her satchel, she went up on tiptoe and gave him a kiss on the mouth. Her bodily warmth reached out for him. Her lips tasted fresh. That might have been her natural flavor but he was guessing that she'd just had a mint, which meant that she'd planned for this kiss.

She went flat-footed and stood, looking up at him.

"That was nice," he said.

"Wait until I pay you back for the massage," she said. "I don't mean to brag, but I'm kind of an expert when it comes to relaxation techniques. I'll start with your feet and work my way up."

"You're killing me."

"And I have scented oils."

He picked up her backpack and followed her to the front door. If they didn't make love soon, he was going to melt into a puddle of pure frustration.

# Chapter Sixteen

*Thursday, 10:30 a.m.*

The morning sunlight beamed through the windshield. A warm day, it felt like spring. Though Kelly had been able to catch a couple of catnaps during Daisy's nine-hour labor, she was exhausted as she drove her van to Nick's condo. When she arrived, one of the professional security men gave her a key and carried her bags to the door. In addition to being stern and imposing, the bodyguard was, as Nick had promised, wearing a shoulder holster.

Outside the door to the condo, he asked, "Should I come inside?"

"Is that what you usually do?"

He gave a curt military nod. "Standard oper-ating procedure is to make sure the premises are secure."

She opened the door wide. "Knock yourself out."

He swept through the two-bedroom condo quickly, poking into the closets and even look-ing under the beds. When he left, he said, "I'll be in the hall. If you need anything, don't hesi-tate to call out."

Alone in Nick's condo, she stood in the hall-way between the two bedrooms, weaving on her feet. She was going to collapse, that was for sure, but she couldn't decide whether she should flop down on Nick's king-size bed or go to the guest bedroom. She peeked into his masculine room, decorated in a faded blue that reminded her of well-worn denim. The bed was made, but the pillow had a dent as though Nick had been lying on top of the covers, looking up at the ceiling. It seemed right to wait for him in here.

She stretched out on his bed with her head on his pillow. It smelled like him, and she snuggled into the covers. She should have been here last night, lying beside him. They should have made love.

Her cell phone started ringing, and she groaned at the sound. If the caller happened to be another pregnant woman going into labor, Kelly would need an intravenous caffeine drip to stay awake.

"Hello?"

"Don't hang up on me."

"Ted?" She bolted upright on the bed and glared at the phone. Was she already asleep and having a nightmare? "What do you want?"

"You need to be reasonable, Kelly. Your stupid accusations are hurting my career. Even if it was years ago, marital infidelity is one of those hot-button issues, and I can't afford a scandal. Do you understand what I'm saying?"

"Are you blaming me for that blog?"

"Of course, it's your fault. Who else would

give a damn about what happened in my first marriage?"

That was what she'd become to him—his first marriage, a blip in his otherwise meteoric rise to power. "Apparently, Ted, you care. You're all worked up about it."

"Just keep your mouth shut. Do you think you can do that?"

She started to defend herself, explaining that she couldn't have informed the blogger about his extramarital affairs because she hadn't known about them. But there was no need to justify her actions. "I've done nothing wrong."

"Let's not get into a he-said-she-said situation. It's an embarrassment. I won't have you bad-mouthing me to the media."

"Don't tell me what to do, Ted."

"What?"

"You're the one who cheated. If there's anyone to blame, it's you, not me."

He cleared his throat. "This doesn't sound like you. When we were married you were—"

"A doormat," she said, finishing his sentence. "Kelly, listen to me."

"It's your turn to listen," she said. "I've changed. I have a life, a career I love and a million possibilities for the future. You mean nothing to me. Goodbye for the last time. I never want to speak to you again."

She disconnected the call and stretched out on the bed. That conversation counted as a triumph. She'd faced her demons from the past, looked them in the eye and seen that they weren't so big and scary, after all. Finally, her first marriage was well and truly ended, unable to hurt her anymore.

Within minutes, she was sound asleep.

A STRANGE AWARENESS invaded her dream state, like a curtain slowly rising or a melody that gradually increased in volume, telling her it was time to wake up. But she was still tired, and the bed was so warm and cozy. She burrowed into the pillow.

There was a fluttering. *Am I being attacked by butterflies?* She tried to bat at the multicolored gossamer wings, but it was no use. She had to wake up.

When she opened her eyes, she was looking into Nick Spencer's handsome face. His cobalt-blue eyes peered through his thick black lashes. He lay beside her on the bed, watching her.

"When you're starting to wake up," he said, "you make noises."

"I don't snore, do I?"

"It's like a kitten. And you wrinkle your nose. Cute, and a little weird." He grinned. "I would have let you sleep, but it's after four o'clock, and I thought you might want to take a shower before the Lamaze class."

She stretched and yawned. "Am I gross and dirty?"

"Why don't we take off your clothes and find out?"

"On second thought, a shower sounds like a fine idea. And food?"

"You'll be pleased to hear that I picked up some basic supplies before I came home." He stroked her hair off her forehead. "Tell me about Daisy's baby."

"Gorgeous little girl with peach-fuzz hair. Seven pounds, eight ounces. Perfectly healthy. The labor went on for nearly nine hours, but it wasn't rough. Daisy and her husband could have handled the first seven hours by themselves, but they were nervous and wanted me there."

"What do you do afterward?"

"I check the baby out and fill out the birth certificate, and then I usually wait until the mother is comfortable with breast feeding." Remembering, she smiled. "Daisy looked so happy with her newborn at her breast."

"You love your work."

"It's the perfect job," she said. "And what have you been up to today?"

"Go ahead and get cleaned up. I'll fill you in on the way to class."

Mindful of the time, Kelly hurried through

her shower and washed her hair. She didn't want to be late, and she was eager to tell the other couples in the Lamaze class about Daisy's baby and show them the photos on her cell phone. After a quick blow-dry and a dab of makeup to cover the dark circles under her eyes, she slipped into a long-sleeved turquoise T-shirt and black yoga pants.

She bounded into the living room. "I'm ready."

"You're dressed for a workout. What kind of exercises am I going to be doing with Lauren tonight?"

"Nothing too strenuous." She had some concerns about Lauren. "When does her husband get back in town?"

"Tomorrow. Why?"

"When I saw her yesterday, she was carrying her baby lower and looked like she might go into labor at any time. I'm glad your brother will be back in time for the birth."

"He never should have scheduled a trip to the other side of the globe so close to Lauren's due date. Jared doesn't get it. He doesn't yet understand what it means to be a father, how much his life is going to change."

"He'll figure it out soon enough."

"No doubt. Then he can dedicate himself to being the best father of all time."

She heard the bitterness in his voice. "You and Jared are kind of competitive."

"Ever since we were kids." He led her into the kitchen and pointed to a rotisserie chicken and a container of slaw on the counter. "You've got fifteen minutes to eat."

"A fine dining experience."

She climbed onto a stool at the counter and dug in. A few bites of protein would pump up her energy. When he placed a glass of water beside her, she chugged half of it.

"How were the bodyguards?" he asked.

"So discreet that they were almost invisible. I noticed their car at the curb, and that was the only hint that they were there. If they were patrolling around the house, they were totally silent. Are they former military?"

"I'm not sure. O'Shea makes the arrangements when we need security." He rested his elbows on the counter and leaned toward her. "I missed you today."

She was glad to hear it. "Tell me how you missed me."

"I was spending a lot of time in offices, listening to endless lectures from Marian and Rod about spreadsheets and balances and business. After a while, their yakking turns into a meaningless drone. It would have been nice to look over and see you sitting there, nodding politely and pretending to pay attention."

"You want to use me as a diversion?" She tore into the chicken breast.

"And a sounding board. Things make more sense when I talk them over with you."

Again, she was complimented. She really liked the way their relationship was growing. "What do you want to talk to me about?"

"Uncle Samuel's will."

WHEN THEY WERE IN HIS SUV headed to the Spencer Building, Nick launched into an encapsulated version of the terms of the will. Arthur had been wrong about his inheritance. He and his sister weren't left out; they both received substantial funds and properties that were worth hundreds of thousands of dollars. But the stock in Spencer Enterprises was transferred in such a way that Nick and Jared had 45 percent of the shares and the rest went into a central trust.

"Why would your uncle do that?" she asked.

"Most of the control stays with the family, but we have to take other interests into consideration." Nick frowned. "I'm guessing that Rod Esterhauser had a lot to do with the arrangement. I think the guy is an ass, but my uncle trusted him and made him executor."

"What about Julia?"

"Of course she already owns her house, free and clear. And she'll receive a significant monthly pension for the rest of her life."

"If she'd married him, she would have gotten everything."

"Don't worry about Julia. She's well taken care of."

She sensed that there was more he hadn't told her. "I don't know much about business. Is Samuel's will typical?"

"Pretty much, it is. He kept the family holdings intact and granted bequests to the people who were important to him."

"What's bothering you?" she asked.

"I was hoping for something more, something that might be a motive for murder. Samuel revised his will two months ago. At that time, he would have had the loan from Radcliff, but his will doesn't mention it."

"And you haven't been able to trace the funds."

"Not at all. The only indication that Samuel got that money is the documentation from Radcliff."

In the gray of dusk, the silhouette of the Spencer Building rose before them. The lights on the roof shone like eternal flames, and she thought this structure made a fitting tribute to the imagination and creativity of Samuel Spencer. He had the vision to know this office park would be a success when others couldn't see past the ends of their noses.

She asked, "Did the will say anything about the gold mine?"

"Ownership of that property and the kilobars of gold are part of a family trust, which Samuel kept intact. But the gold mine is the best clue we have so far. I think we need to go there and poke around."

"How far away is it? I don't want to leave any of my clients in the lurch."

"It's an hour and a half drive, but I could arrange for a private chopper."

"I'd love a trip to the mountains." She kept forgetting that Nick Spencer was a very rich man. He didn't wear his wealth like a crown, but the cash was there when he wanted it. "The only other time I've been on a helicopter was a Flight for Life situation, bringing a pregnant woman with complications to a hospital. It wasn't a good time."

"How did it turn out?"

"After the ob-gyn performed an emergency C-section, the mom and baby were fine."

Outside the Spencer Building, she noticed the reporter who had written the blog. She really ought to thank the guy. His intrusive behavior provided the final nudge that pushed her over the edge and set her free.

As she'd expected, the other four couples in the Lamaze class loved the photos she'd taken of Daisy and listened avidly as she described the nine-hour labor.

"That's not an unusual length of time," Kelly said. "It sounds daunting, but you're not in constant pain. The hard part comes at the end."

"That's when you've got to squeeze a watermelon through a straw," Roxanne said.

"Let's try to come up with a better image," Kelly said. "In addition to the physical part of labor, having a baby is one of the most emotional experiences you'll ever have. Get comfortable. We're going to do some visualization."

As she led the class through a positive imagination exercise, Kelly went to her own happy place—Nick's bedroom. To the class, she said, "Close your eyes and use all your senses. Think beyond what you see. What's your favorite scent?"

"Clean laundry," said one woman.

"Fresh pie," Lauren chimed in.

In Kelly's imagination, she took a whiff of the toasty smell she associated with Nick. Licking her lips, she tasted his kiss. When she opened her eyes and peeked, she saw him watching her. His blue eyes were compelling. She could hardly wait for the class to be over so she could make her imaginings into reality.

# Chapter Seventeen

*Thursday, 8:22 p.m.*

As soon as they said good-night to the class and closed up the room, Kelly and Nick bolted. Their separate minds had wrapped around a single thought, and they were both ready, so ready, to make love.

In his SUV, she said, "My happy place was you."

"I'm with you," he said. "I started with thinking about you in the outdoors with the wind in your hair and flowers all around you. And then the wind blew harder, and your clothes went flying off."

"That's handy."

"You said to use all your senses, so I added a sound track. I tried for something ethereal, like a flute or a harp. But I'm a country-western boy. So, I heard guitars and the sweet voice of Taylor Swift."

He paused, and she had to ask, "Then what?"

"I had to shut down my imagination before I got too turned on. I was going to be cradling my pregnant sister-in-law in my arms, and I didn't want her to get the wrong idea."

She chuckled as he pulled his SUV into the parking lot outside the condo. She didn't wait for him to come around to her side and open the door. There wasn't time to be polite, wasn't time for anything. The kissing started in the elevator as they rode to the third floor. By the time he unlocked his door, he'd already taken off her jacket and had his hands under her shirt.

Inside the condo, he stepped back and held her by the shoulders as he looked into her eyes. "I don't want to rush."

"Neither do I." But adrenaline pumped through her, sending her pulse into high gear.

"Would you like wine?"

"That sounds very civilized."

"Too civilized," he said as he led the way down the hall to his bedroom. "I'm going to leave you here while I get the wine."

"What am I supposed to do?"

"Surprise me."

She was so eager to make love that she didn't need encouragement. Kelly had never really thought of herself as a sexy woman. Making love had always been natural for her and, most of the time, enjoyable. But she didn't have the confidence to be a sultry femme fatale...not until now.

Kelly had changed. She was a different woman.

In his bedroom, she abandoned all thoughts of self-consciousness and stripped down to her bra and panties. It would have been great if her underwear had been lacy and black, but the simple beige brassiere made it look as if she wasn't wearing anything at all, and her bikini-cut panties were bright pink. With luck, she wouldn't be wearing them for long.

She pulled the comforter off his bed and slid between the smooth yellow sheets. As she waited for him, a tiny doubt bubbled up in her mind. Was there a future for this relationship? He lived in Breckenridge, and she was basically homeless. It was entirely possible that they would only have a few days together, maybe a week or a month. Was she okay with that?

When he walked through the bedroom door holding a wine bottle and two glasses and wearing nothing but a pair of black briefs, she decided she was fine with things the way they were. No commitment was necessary. If tonight was all they had, it would be enough.

Not taking her eyes off him, she lay back on the pillow. "I like your outfit, Nick."

"Same to you." He sat on the edge of the bed and set down the wine and stemmed glasses on the bedside table. "But I'd like it better if we got this sheet out of the way."

He yanked the material aside, revealing her whole body and her resplendent pink panties. His gaze was warm as he slowly looked her up and down, and she arched her back, shamelessly posing like a cover girl. "Is this what you imagined?"

"Everything and a bag of chips."

He slipped his arm under her back and lifted her off the sheets, placing her in his lap. She knew that simple move required some serious muscles, enough to bench press her entire weight. She remembered in Julia's house when he lifted her off the staircase. His strength was impressive.

On his lap with her arms draped around his shoulders, she kissed him slowly and thoroughly. First, they tasted each other. Next, they tried the wine. A sip of Chardonnay aroused her palate and slithered down her throat. No need to worry about getting drunk, she was already intoxicated by his nearness.

"Tomorrow," she said, "we'll go to the mountains."

"I know a little place we can stay overnight."

"Camping?" She enjoyed roughing it, cooking over a fire and sleeping under the stars.

"The Hearthstone Motel," he said, "the place where my uncle stayed when he visited the gold mine."

No matter how much she wished otherwise, Samuel's murder was never far from his thoughts. It was a wound that she couldn't heal for him. All she could do was offer comfort.

After they finished a glass of wine, he stretched her out on the bed. Instead of lying beside her, he went to the end of the mattress.

"The first time I saw you," he said, "I noticed your crazy-colored toenails—pink, yellow and purple."

"It's a game I was playing with Princess Butterfly."

"This is what I wanted to do to those toes."

He picked up her foot, caressed each toe and massaged the arch. His touch set off a chain reaction in her nervous system, elevating her sensitivity. He reached up her calves and then went higher. Excitement rippled across the surface of her skin in waves that grew stronger and stronger.

Gasping, she said, "If this is the start to the massage you promised, keep going."

His calloused hands climbed her torso. When he finally touched her breasts, the anticipation was too much for her to stand. She pulled him down on top of her. She needed him, needed to feel him inside her, and couldn't wait another moment.

He matched her passion and encouraged her to go even higher. In a barely controlled frenzy, they made love.

Later that night, she paid him back, using massage techniques she'd read about when looking into Tantric Yoga. "I always wanted to take a class in this," she said, "but it's a couples' thing."

"Sign us up."

She'd never been this daring in the bedroom, gazing into his eyes and touching him intimately. The release of sexual energy was amazing. She'd heard about nine thrusts to ecstasy, and Nick delivered.

*Friday, 10:04 a.m.*

THE NEXT MORNING, NICK took his time getting out of bed, which meant he made love to Kelly again. Though he couldn't forget the questions, sadness and even the danger that plagued him, he felt good. Being with her made this one of the best days in his life, better than the Christmas when he got a puppy and better than his sixteenth birthday when he lost his virginity.

While she was in the shower, he lay back on the bed and savored the sweetness. His day was bound to get worse.

Kelly poked her head out of the bathroom door. "When do we go to the mountains?"

"First we've got to stop by Jared's house. He got home this morning at eight o'clock."

He wasn't looking forward to facing off with his brother. They should have been united by grief, but they had different opinions about Samuel. Jared didn't appreciate their uncle's creativity when it meant a lack of concern about the bottom line, and he blamed their uncle for putting the company in the red.

Over the years, Nick's relationship with his brother had become more about finance and less about family. Jared couldn't forget, not for a minute, that he was the chief executive officer. He was going to be seriously ticked off about the Radcliff loan and Nick's determination to pay it off. Marian and Rod had already made their position clear, and he expected Jared to follow the corporate line.

An hour later, Nick drove his SUV into the cul-de-sac where he grew up. Unlike the scene a couple of nights ago, there were no cars parked in Jared's circular driveway.

"It seems too quiet," Kelly said. "Where did everybody go?"

He noticed several cars parked along the curb and down the street. Standing at the front door was a plainclothes security guard.

"Traffic control," he said. "Security is keeping the driveway open and the media held back. It's not a bad idea."

Still, he drove his SUV into the driveway, stopped and threw the gear into Park. Before the guard could order him to move on, he was out of the driver's seat and coming around to Kelly's side to open her door.

"Sir," the guard said, "I have to ask you to move your vehicle."

"I'm only going to be here for a couple of minutes," Nick said. "It's okay."

"I have my orders, sir. If you give me your keys, I'll move the vehicle for you."

"You don't have to valet for me. It's really okay."

As far as Nick was concerned, this rule didn't apply to him. Though this was Jared's house now, Nick had lived here for nearly fifteen years. Nobody had the right to tell him where he could and couldn't park.

He opened the door for Kelly and helped her out of the car while the security guard talked into a tiny microphone attached to an earpiece. Nick almost hoped for a physical confrontation with this hard-bodied guy. It would ease his tension to punch something.

The front door opened, and Jared stepped outside. The most obvious physical difference between them was size. Nick stood about six inches taller. When they were growing up, he'd passed Jared in height just after his ninth birthday. His brother had never forgiven him.

Jared said, "I really wish you'd move your SUV."

"Are you going to make me?" Nick was fully

aware that he was being as immature as a nine-year-old, and he didn't care.

"Fine." After a long-suffering sigh, Jared spoke to the guard. "It's all right for him to park here."

Immediately, Nick felt guilty. Jared looked tired. His eyes were bloodshot, and his usually healthy complexion looked wan and pale. Either the trip from Singapore had been rough or he was actually feeling something about the death of their uncle.

Giving him the benefit of the doubt, Nick assumed the latter. He held open his arms and gave his brother a hug. "How are you holding up?"

"I can't believe Samuel is gone."

They'd gone through the death of their father together when Nick was twenty-six. Losing him to a sudden heart attack had been hard; there were so many things Nick wished he'd taken the time to tell his dad. He hadn't made that mistake with Samuel. He and his uncle had built a lot of memories.

He introduced his brother to Kelly, and they went inside. The atmosphere was more subdued than yesterday. Lauren sat in the living room beside a cousin Nick barely remembered. Julia was in the kitchen with two other women. He wondered if she'd spoken to her son.

Jared took him through the French doors into the enclosed porch where Nick had gone with Julia to find some privacy. His brother left the door ajar. "Fill me in, Nick. Was it murder or suicide?"

"I don't know how it was done or why, but he didn't kill himself."

"The police don't agree with you. The only tangible piece of evidence is that Samuel was left-handed."

"The police didn't know him. Samuel wasn't depressed, and he would never leave a note that said he was sorry. The man never apologized for anything in his life."

"You're right about that." Jared pulled one of the chairs out from the table but didn't sit. "Samuel's weird decisions have cost us a boatload of money."

"That's according to Marian's accounting system," Nick said. "Samuel had vision. Projects that look like losers are going to pay off in the long run. I went over the terms of his will with Rod yesterday, and it's all in order."

"Why wouldn't it be?"

"It's not important." Nick hated that they were talking about money. Their uncle had died. They should be supporting each other, dealing with the pain.

"I'll decide if it's important or not." His tone was sharp. "What kind of problem did you expect with the will?"

"I talked to Arthur Starkey. He thought he was going to inherit big, but he was wrong."

"Thank God for that. If our uncle had given all his money to Arthur, I would have believed that he'd gone off the rails and killed himself."

Nick glanced at the French doors, wondering if Julia could overhear what they were saying. "I'm going to take off soon. There's a lead I want to follow up on."

"Is this about the million-dollar loan?"

"Yes."

"Damn it, Nick." Jared rolled his eyes like a teenager. When they were together, they tended to revert to their younger selves. "You've got to give up on this. Samuel was crazy to borrow money from Barry Radcliff. And you're crazy to follow up on it. Leave it to the courts to decide."

"What if the courts decide we have to pay with the Valiant gold? That's what Radcliff wants. According to his document, which is signed by our uncle, he could be collecting the gold next week."

"That's not going to happen," Jared said. "We'll fight it. We'll negotiate our way out of the problem."

"What about doing the right thing? Samuel

made a deal with Radcliff, fair and square. We should honor his intention."

"Don't pretend that you're taking the high road." Jared jabbed a finger at his chest. "You're irresponsible. If you were involved with the day-to-day business, you'd understand."

Nick had come here expecting a fight and had gotten one. Anger twisted in his gut. Nobody got to him the way Jared did. He could handle arguments with Marian or Rod or even Julia; he could even put up with insults from Arthur. But Jared made his blood boil.

He needed to get out of here before he did something stupid. He pivoted. "I'll keep you informed."

"You do that," Jared said. "Tell me all about your wild-goose chase. I could use a laugh."

When he stalked through the house, Kelly had her purse in hand and immediately fell into step beside him. It was as though she'd been waiting for him.

He was in his SUV and driving away before

he was in control enough to speak. "Did you hear any of that?"

"I heard all of it," she said. "You were yelling at each other."

Nick hadn't been aware of raising his voice. He was losing it.

## Chapter Eighteen

*Friday, 2:15 p.m.*

The chopper ride into the mountains did a lot to improve Nick's mood. His attitude toward flight was jaded; he used the helicopter charter service often to get to job sites and check out new properties. But he enjoyed this trip because Kelly was having so much fun, pressing her nose against the window, pointing, grinning and sighting a family of elk from the air.

When they landed at an unmanned airfield near Hearthstone, a fully gassed SUV stood ready and waiting. He tossed their bags in the back, got behind the steering wheel and set their course on the navigational system. The Valiant gold mine didn't have an address, so he had to use county routes that would bring them close.

"I could get used to this," she said. "Flying from place to place, having everything ready and waiting when you arrive. I can't believe you arranged all this with one phone call."

"I'm a frequent traveler," he said. "Working in the mountains means I cover a lot of territory. It's efficient to take a chopper."

"If I need to get back to Valiant in a hurry, how long will it take the pilot to respond?"

"I've got him on speed dial. I guarantee you won't be late for a birth." He drove away from the airfield onto a main road. "We're going to the mine first. There's not a lot of daylight left and I don't want to be climbing around in the dark."

"How long has it been since the mine was operational?"

"The last time a Spencer took gold out of this hole in the ground was around World War II.

That was in my grandpa's day. He was the last of the real gold miners in the family, and he never believed that the mine was played out. He thought the next big strike was just a few feet deeper or in a different direction."

"He sounds like a gambler."

"I guess he was. He liked to dream."

"That's the Spencer heritage," she said. "You're a dreamer, and so was your uncle."

But the dreamers weren't calling the shots. Spencer Enterprises had taken a different direction when they diversified into property sales and construction—a safer way to earn a buck than prospecting for gold. His father had marched them down that path and Jared continued his tradition.

Even though he'd cooled off, Nick couldn't understand his brother's endless focus on profit. Jared had devoted less than five minutes to mourning Samuel before he started talking about the bottom line and irresponsible spending.

"This is beautiful," she said. "I love the mountains."

"Enough to stay in Colorado?"

"Oh, I'm staying. My scumbag ex-husband isn't going to chase me away again. But I'm not sure whether I want to stay in Valiant and work with Serena. I could join an established clinic in Denver. Or I could even start my own midwife practice in the mountains."

"Maybe in Breckenridge," he said as he turned off the main road into a rocky canyon.

"That's your backyard," she said. "Do you know if there are other midwives in your area?"

"I couldn't say."

It seemed odd to think of birthing babies as a business venture, but that was exactly what it was. Midwives weren't entrepreneurs, but they were self-employed businesswomen and had to take the competition into consideration.

The unspoken question about Breckenridge was whether she wanted to be near him on a regular basis. After last night, he knew that he wanted to be with her…for a while. He couldn't say how long. When they first met, Nick had been looking for a distraction, not a mate. He wasn't sure if he was ready for a commitment.

The squiggly line on the navigational system pointed toward a road that wasn't there. "I'm not sure if we're going in the right direction. I haven't been up here in years."

Kelly leaned toward the windshield and squinted into the distance. "It looks like there's a turn about twenty yards farther."

He took her suggestion. After they'd gone about a mile on the one-lane gravel road, he began to recognize the surroundings. On his right was a towering granite wall. On the left, the terrain was less rugged. A narrow creek rippled at the side of the road.

Though it was chilly, he put down his window and inhaled the mountain air. Even if they didn't find a clue, he was glad they'd come here. The mountains fulfilled a primal need in his soul. Having Kelly with him made it even better.

After another few miles, he turned off the GPS navigation. His memory was a better guide. After a few more turns, he parked at the base of a hill. "We have to walk from here."

"No problem. I wore my hiking boots." She bounded out of the SUV and came toward him, hopping from one foot to the other. "I forgot how comfortable these are. I hardly ever wore them when I was in Texas. Different place, different shoes."

He crossed the creek and found the well-worn path that led to the mine. "This used to have a narrow track for ore carts. You can still see some of the weathered planks they used for ties."

She hiked beside him, and they gradually ascended the rugged hillside. "How did they get the ore carts back to the top? Going downhill was easy. But back up?"

"The ore was emptied out at the bottom, so the carts weren't as heavy. I think they used mules."

The closer they got to the mine, the more of the wooden ties were in place. All the metal tracks were gone.

"Great view," she said.

He had to agree. A thick forest of conifers, pines and evergreens were spread across rolling hills and jagged rock formations. In the far distance, he could see snow-capped peaks.

They circled a huge boulder and were at the boarded-up entrance to the mine shaft. There was nothing to indicate that this was the famous Valiant mine, one of the richest strikes in the Rocky Mountains. The posted signs said: Danger. No Trespassing. Keep Out.

"I've only been inside once," he said. "My dad pulled open some of the boards and we climbed through the hole. I couldn't have been more than seven or eight, and I thought the mine was really cool. My dad turned off the flashlight, and we were in total darkness. You couldn't see your hand when it was right in front of your face."

"Bringing a flashlight would have been smart," she said.

"Why? We're not going inside."

"Somebody else has."

Behind one of the heavy weathered boards that blocked the entrance was a piece of plywood that looked new. The nails that held it in place were still shiny. When he pulled on the old board, the whole piece came away, creating an opening that was wide enough to slip through.

The discovery gave him hope. They might actually find a useful clue. "My uncle must have been here."

"Why?"

"I don't know, but if we retrace his path we've got to find something."

She took out her cell phone and turned on the light function. "This isn't real bright, but it's better than nothing."

He loved that she was adventurous enough

to follow him into a deserted mine shaft. "Not afraid of the dark?"

"The dark doesn't bother me, but I have to warn you that I hate bats. If we run into any of those ugly little beasts, prepare to hear me scream."

Using his own cell phone for light, he wedged his body through the narrow opening into a space that was about twelve feet wide. The walls were rough-hewn rock, and the ceiling was just high enough for him to stand upright without stooping.

The glow from their cell phones barely penetrated the thick, heavy darkness. He had the same eager, excited feeling he'd had when he was a kid. This was incredibly cool.

"What are we looking for?" she asked. Her voice was calm, but he noticed that she'd latched on to his jacket and attached herself like Velcro to his side.

"I'm trying to think like my uncle." He stooped and ran the light from his cell across the stone floor, looking for footprints. "Why would he come here? He had to be looking for something."

"Buried treasure," she said.

"Not likely."

"Why not? Buried treasure fits with your family history."

"The Spencers were prospectors," he said, "not pirates."

"Think about it. The gold that was mined out of here is like treasure."

"Are you making a point?" he asked.

"I actually think I am," she said. "There's only one reason to come to a gold mine, and that's gold."

He followed her logic. "Samuel came here because he was considering opening the mining operations again, and he needed information."

"What kind of information?"

"I know that you take ore samples for testing to assayers. I don't know much about it."

"There are plenty of experts," she said. "The School of Mines is right outside Denver."

They went deeper into the mine, finding where it narrowed into a corridor. Nick stopped. Beyond this point, the footing got dangerous. Long ago, his father had warned him about mine shafts, holes in the floor that went straight down. "Without the right equipment, we shouldn't go any deeper."

"Good." She pressed up against him. "I don't want you to think I'm scared, but I'm kind of creeped out. It's so dark. I feel like I'm inside a shadow."

He pulled her into his arms and held her close. Without her support and encouragement, he might have given up on following the trail that had led to this point. He might never have known what his uncle was doing. "Thanks for sticking with me."

She held up her cell so he could see her smile. "Like glue."

"Let's get out of here."

Coming into the fresh mountain air after being in the mine felt like a rebirth. After replacing the boards that blocked the entrance, they headed back to the SUV. Daylight was scarce in the canyon, and shadows had already darkened the western wall.

Driving back toward the tiny town nearest the mine, he tried to think like his uncle. For the past six quarters, Spencer Enterprises had been in financial trouble. Marian had been vetoing Samuel's ideas for new construction projects. "He was trying to help, thinking outside the box."

"The price of gold keeps going up and up," she said. "Opening the mine might be profitable."

"And he borrowed the money from Radcliff to test out his theory before presenting it. A million sounds excessive. It wouldn't take that much to run some tests and talk to the experts."

His theory had a lot of holes, but it was the best he could come up with. He continued,

"Even if Samuel was making plans for opening the mine, it doesn't explain why he was so secretive about it. He's always relied on Julia for research and information. Why wouldn't he tell her?"

"That seems like a troubled relationship," she said.

"It's just their way." Samuel and Julia had been together for so long, he couldn't imagine them being separated. "The two of them like to bicker."

"I don't know them the way you do, but I know what it's like when a woman falls out of love. The light goes out in her eyes. Her voice turns cold when she says his name."

"Is that what you see in Julia?"

Kelly nodded. "Whenever she talks about Samuel, she sounds angry. It's almost like he betrayed her."

"Maybe he did. Arthur didn't get what he wanted in the will. Julia might have been expecting more." She'd been with Samuel for more than thirty years. If he pulled the rug out from under her and cut her inheritance, she'd be mad. "She deserved more."

"A better question," Kelly said, "is why didn't your uncle tell you?"

She was right. Nick was the logical person for Samuel to confide in. Why hadn't his uncle come to him? He could tell himself that they were both too busy, but it was a lousy excuse. If Samuel had wanted to talk, a drive to Breckenridge wasn't too far to deter him. All it would have taken was an invitation from him to have Nick meet him in Valiant or at the gold mine.

His high hopes for a solution slipped down a few notches. He didn't want to think they were on the wrong path, but it was possible. If only there was something tangible…a sign.

He drove to the edge of the town that consisted of a tavern, a tiny grocery store with an attached gas pump, a motel and a couple of houses. If you blinked, you might drive by without noticing the town existed.

"I'm surprised there's a motel," she said. "This doesn't look like a place that gets many visitors."

He guided the SUV into the motel parking lot where there were no other vehicles. The log building was shaped like a long shoebox with six numbered doors in a row. The sidewalk in front had been recently swept, but the more important upkeep—like painting the eaves and repairing a section of roof that looked damaged—hadn't been done. "This place has been here for a long time. Maybe even before World War II when there were miners who needed rooms."

Outside the office, there was a wooden carved sign with the name of the motel. Nick repeated the word to himself. "Hearthstone, hearthstone."

"Heart of stone," she said.

Samuel's last words had significance after all. *Heart of stone.* He'd been telling them to come here.

# Chapter Nineteen

*Friday, 4:52 p.m.*

As soon as Kelly walked through the door, the plump woman in the motel office greeted her with a huge, friendly smile and introduced herself as Dora. She turned down the volume on the television that was across from her easy chair and went behind a small desk. "Do you have reservations?"

It seemed unlikely that anyone had reserved a room at the Hearthstone Motel in the past few decades, but Kelly was polite. "We're here on the spur of the minute. Do you have a room?"

"I'll put you at the very end so you can have

some privacy. You picked a good weekend to visit. The weather is supposed to be grand."

Nick slid a hundred-dollar bill across her desk. "In addition to the room, we're looking for some information. Can you help us?"

The hundred quickly disappeared into Dora's ample cleavage. "I'd be happy to help you out."

"My uncle stayed with you a couple of times in the last few months. He's an older man, tall and skinny. His name is Samuel Spencer."

"Oh, my, yes, I remember. There's all kinds of stuff about him on the television. The police don't know if he killed himself or was murdered. A terrible thing."

"Isn't it?" Kelly figured that Dora's life revolved around the television set. Though she'd turned down the volume, she'd left the picture on. "It's just like those crime shows. We're looking for a murderer, and we need to know everything you can tell us about Samuel Spencer."

"This is about the woman, isn't it? He met her at the tavern. When I saw them together, I thought he was old enough to be her father, but she came closer, and she had plenty of lines on her pretty face. I think they were lovers."

Kelly was tempted to turn around and give Nick a big, fat "I told you so." She'd seen the signs of trouble in Samuel and Julia's relationship, and she was becoming a bit of an expert on infidelity. Keeping her focus on Dora, she asked, "Did you happen to get her name?"

"Not the first time she met him," Dora said. "On another time, she was the first to arrive and made the room reservation. If it'll help, I can go through my records and dig up her credit card information."

"We'd appreciate it," Nick said.

Dora took a metal file box from her lower desk drawer, opened it and started thumbing through receipts. In less than a minute, she found what she was looking for. She read the name. "Virginia L. Hancock."

Kelly thanked her warmly. Chatty little Dora

had given them a real lead to follow. "Is there anything else you can tell us?"

"You aren't the first people who came looking for information about Mr. Spencer. A couple of weeks ago, there was a private investigator. He had pure white hair."

"Trask."

AFTER PROMISING DORA that they would come back for the room and paying her another hundred, they went back to the SUV. Kelly was beside herself with excitement. "Do you think Dora is right? Did Samuel have a lover?"

"He was close to seventy," Nick said. "That doesn't mean he wasn't still interested in the ladies. I still can't see him doing this to Julia."

Kelly decided that saying "I told you so" would be mean. Nick wanted to keep a good opinion of his uncle. "Do you think we can find Ms. Hancock?"

He took his laptop from his overnight bag. After about five minutes of searching, he had an address and phone number for Virginia L. Hancock. She lived near Silverton, about twenty miles away from Hearthstone.

"She doesn't have a website," he said, "but there's a brief bio. She's a professor, retired. And she used to work at the Colorado School of Mines."

While they drove, she realized that she was doing most of the talking. Nick seemed withdrawn, as though he was rethinking his opinion of the uncle he'd loved and trusted. Finally, he said, "I can't believe Samuel cheated."

"Technically," she said, "he and Julia were never married."

"But he made a commitment to her. He built her that incredible house."

She liked that he had strong feelings about standing by his commitments. One of the first things he'd said to her was that she needed to be honest with him. She had to tell him the truth to earn his trust. "You're a puzzling man, Nick Spencer. People keep saying that you're irresponsible, but it's the opposite. You never break your word."

"Yeah, I'm a real Boy Scout."

"You'd look cute in one of those uniforms with the short pants."

"Cute?" He scoffed. "No man likes being described as cute."

"If I said what I really thought about you, we'd have to pull over and make love right now."

"You know I'd like that, but not right now. We're so close to finding out why my uncle was murdered. Let's hope Virginia L. Hancock has the answers we need."

The GPS navigational system proved invaluable in locating Ms. Hancock's secluded cabin in the forest. Her name on the mailbox told them they'd come to the right place, but not at the right time. All the lights were off. It didn't look as if anybody was home.

The fact that she wasn't here didn't stop Nick. As soon as he parked by her front door, he was out of the SUV and climbing the four stairs to a covered porch that wrapped around the front and one of the sides of the cedar structure. He rapped on the door. "Ms. Hancock? Are you here?"

Kelly crept up the stairs behind him. This felt like an intrusion, even more so when Nick turned the handle and walked into the house. She stopped short at the door. "You can't do this. It's breaking and entering."

"It's entering," he clarified. "The door was unlocked so I didn't have to break anything."

"We're going to be in so much trouble."

Still, she followed him inside, turning on lights as she went. The front room of the house was half sitting area and half office, with a huge, cluttered desk and files spilling in every direction. Whatever Ms. Hancock's talents were, housekeeping wasn't one of them. In the kitchen, her dishes were washed and stacked in a dish rack but not put away in the cabinets. In the large bedroom, clothes were tossed across chairs and several pairs of shoes looked as though they'd been left where she walked out of them. The clutter extended to more than dirty laundry. "Nick, come in here."

He appeared in the doorway. "What did you find?"

She pointed to a table by the dresser where it appeared that Ms. Hancock had been cleaning her rifle, make that two rifles. There were three other handguns. "I don't think we want to make this woman angry."

"But we might want to be prepared to meet her." He picked up a .45 caliber automatic and checked the clip. "Fully loaded."

"Put that down."

But he carried the gun with him into the front room where he scooped a couple of magazines off the sofa before sprawling across it. "We don't have a listing for her cell phone. It seems like the only thing we can do is wait for her to come home."

Kelly hated this plan. If the woman who lived here came home and found intruders, she'd be justified in blasting them into next week. Colorado had the "Make My Day" law that gave homeowners the right to shoot trespassers without fear of prosecution. "We should wait in the car."

"Why not be comfortable?"

She went back through the house, turning off lights. When she got to the living room, she flipped the switch and darkness fell around them. "Come on, Nick. I'm serious about this. A woman living alone with lots of guns isn't somebody to mess around with."

He grumbled as he got to his feet. "The SUV isn't comfortable enough to sleep in. What if she doesn't come back until morning?"

"For a Boy Scout, you have a real bad attitude."

When she opened the front door, she thought she saw someone near the SUV. "Ms. Hancock? Is that you?"

Nick grabbed her arm and pulled her back

inside. Half a second later, she heard a blast of gunfire. Her worst fear had been realized.

Crouched on the floor beside him, she asked, "What do we do now?"

He moved to the window, stood and peeked around the edge. In a low voice, he said, "Bring me the rifles and the other handgun."

"You can't shoot at her. She thinks she's defending her property."

He ducked in time to avoid being hit by several bullets that shattered the window. Rising, he poked the automatic through the broken pane and returned fire.

Staying away from the window, Kelly shouted, "Hold your fire, Ms. Hancock. We don't mean you any harm."

"Save your breath," Nick said. "I can see the shooter, and it's not a woman. Kelly, get the guns."

She darted through the house to the bedroom and armed herself. She hadn't fired a rifle in a long time, so she figured she'd be better off using one of the handguns.

There was more gunfire at the front of the house. She went toward Nick, who was standing beside the window, trying to look out. "He's behind the SUV. I don't want to disable our vehicle."

She passed him the rifle. "Are you any good with one of these?"

"I'm better with a bow, but I might make this shot."

"What should I do?"

"Go to the other window and lay down some fire to attract his attention."

She scooted across the room and got into position. On the other side of the room, she saw Nick take a knee and sight through the lower part of the window. "Now," he said.

Shooting blindly, she blasted through the window and pulled her hand back. Nick got off two shots.

"Did you hit him?" she asked.

"I can't tell."

There was more gunfire outside, an exchange of gunfire. Kelly heard the distinct sound of two different guns. But no shots were being fired at the house. And then, there was silence.

A woman's voice called out, "People in my house, identify yourself."

"I'm Nick Spencer. You knew my uncle."

"Stay where you are. I'm coming in."

The door opened and a woman stepped through. She had a gun in each hand. "Sorry about your uncle, Nick."

# Chapter Twenty

*Friday, 7:15 p.m.*

The first thing Nick noticed about Virginia Hancock was that she looked nothing like Julia. If his uncle had a type of woman who appealed to him, it wasn't Virginia, who was short, buxom and bursting with energy. She yanked the cap off her head, and thick auburn hair cascaded to her shoulders.

"I chased that bastard off," she said. "He hightailed it out of here in his car. I guess he didn't want to take a chance on fighting off three of us."

Kelly stepped forward and introduced herself.

"I'm really sorry for coming into your house uninvited."

"Don't worry. I've already called the sheriff, but I don't intend to press charges. If you hadn't been here, that guy might have gotten the drop on me."

"Did you get a look at him?" Nick asked.

"It's pretty dark out there, and he was dressed head to toe in black."

Kelly said, "He was wearing a cap so you couldn't tell if he had white hair. Does the name Y. E. Trask mean anything to you?"

"I wish I could help you, but no." She crossed the room, set her handguns on the desk and sat behind it. "I've been expecting to see you, Nick. Did your uncle have a chance to explain what we've been up to before he died?"

Nick wasn't sure he wanted to hear this confession. "He didn't tell me anything."

She clasped her hands behind her neck and leaned back in the swivel chair. "Samuel and I have been busy beavers for the past couple

of months. Sometimes, he'd come here. Sometimes, I'd meet him in that cheesy little motel in
Hearthstone. We had a heck of a good time putting together our plans. Sometimes, we'd talk
all night."

"Plans?" Nick still didn't know what she was
talking about.

"Old Samuel really kept you in the dark." She
looked over at Kelly. "Would you like something to drink? I've got some beer in the fridge."

"A beer sounds great. I'd like to drink until I
forget what just happened. This is the first time
I've been shot at."

"You haven't really lived until you face death."

"About those plans," Nick said.

"I've been retired from teaching for two years,
and I was getting a little bored out here. When
Samuel offered me a chance to take part in the
reopening of the Valiant Mine, I jumped at it."

Nick had been right. His uncle hadn't been
sneaking off to the Hearthstone Motel for an

affair. He wanted to reopen the mine. "Is it a feasible project?" he asked.

"It could very well be," she said. "I've taken ore samples and had them tested with an assayer. We've studied the old maps of the mine, and we've gone in there several times."

That explained the opening in the boarded-up entrance. "How expensive would it be to get the mine operational?"

"Very expensive, make no mistake about that. The old support beams are insufficient to handle the weight of new and improved equipment. And mine safety standards are quite a bit more stringent than they were before World War II. But Samuel had an idea for how he'd pay for it. Let me show you."

While Virginia pulled open her desk drawers and rooted through them, Kelly handed him a cold beer. He chugged half the bottle in a single gulp. His adrenaline was already running high from the gun battle, and he was starting to get excited about the prospect—no pun intended—of reopening the mine.

"Here it is." She held up an envelope with a big green dollar sign on it. "I have here a check for a million dollars. All those zeros are real impressive."

Kelly gasped. "You kept it in your desk? And you don't even lock your front door?"

"The best place to hide things is in plain sight."

Nick took the envelope from her and opened it. "The check was never cashed."

"At first, Samuel made the loan because he thought we might run into some big expenses up front, but he was able to pay for everything out of his own pocket. And then, he figured that man who gave him this money might be willing to invest a lot more."

Nick had a similar impression of Radcliff. "He likes gold."

"Most people do," she said. "But there's significant uranium in that mine, too."

"Stop," Kelly said, holding up her hand. "You're moving too fast for me. How were you going to get him to invest?"

"When it came time for Samuel to pay back the loan, he was going to bring his investor up, show him around and offer him the opportunity to become the next gold baron of Colorado."

Nick finished his beer and sank down onto the sofa. From outside the shattered windows, he heard the approaching sirens of the local sheriff. This felt like one of those moments that could change his life forever. He was standing on the tightrope, not sure if he wanted to take the next step. He looked to Kelly and asked, "Should I?"

"Do it."

A couple of hours ago, his brother said he might be crazy, and Nick wondered if that was true. He was about to take business advice from a midwife. Not exactly the most educated source. But he trusted her more than anyone else, and he'd never felt so sure that he was doing the right thing.

He looked across the room at Virginia. "I like where Samuel was going, and I want to stay on the same path."

He was about to become a gold miner.

*Saturday, 4:45 p.m.*

NICK SPENT LAST NIGHT and most of the day on Saturday going over maps and plans with Virginia. When he'd pegged her as Julia's opposite, he'd been 100 percent correct. Julia was cautious and neat and never would have encouraged Samuel to take a huge risk like this, while Virginia was infuriatingly chaotic and completely unafraid. She and Kelly had rapidly become the best of friends.

Getting started with the mining operation was a matter of logistics. He was accustomed to setting up job sites in the mountains and arranged for a double-wide trailer that would be used as a mobile office on property the Spencers owned near Hearthstone. He told Virginia to hire a staff using her former students at the School of Mines. For now, everybody was required to carry a gun and know how to use it. Until Nick figured out what Trask was up to and who he worked for, they needed to be cautious.

On Saturday evening, he sat on a rocky cliff outside the mine to watch the sunset. Kelly joined him, slipping into the crook of his arm. Tonight, he'd make love to her, and he hoped it wouldn't be the last time. Their budding relationship was about to run into a snag.

As the sun dipped lower and the sky blazed with rich oranges, reds and pinks, he held her chin and kissed her lightly. "It looks like I'll be spending a lot of time up here."

"I know."

"It's a long way from Serena's practice."

"Geographically challenging," she said. "That's what they call it when two people want to be together but are separated by miles. It doesn't really worry me."

"Why is that?"

"You have a chopper service on speed dial." She grinned. "It's probably best that we're not in each others' pocket. When we have a little time apart, we can really appreciate when we're together. And there are reasons for you to see me. We have to be a couple to take that Tantric Yoga class."

He caressed the slender line of her waist and the flare of her hips. "I'd fly in for that."

"Speaking of classes," she said, "I need to get back tomorrow for my Lamaze group."

"I'm coming with you. There's a conversation I need to have with my brother." A talk he wasn't looking forward to. "I don't need to think about that now."

She rested her hand on his jaw and looked him in the eye. "I wish we'd gotten all the answers we came here looking for."

The most important question remained a mystery. He didn't know who killed Samuel or why. Trask was part of that equation, but

Nick couldn't figure how the white-haired man fit into the picture. Sooner or later, it would all make sense.

*Sunday, 5:12 p.m.*

TONIGHT, FOR THE FIRST TIME, Jared would be attending Kelly's Lamaze class with his wife. Nick decided to take advantage of the situation and meet with Jared at the Spencer Building, which was neutral ground for both of them. In Nick's office on the tenth floor, the two brothers squared off.

"I'll go first," Jared said. "I have bad news. The Singapore deal fell through."

His brother wasn't accustomed to failure, and Nick could see the pain in his eyes. "I know you worked hard to put that together."

"If we had that deal, Spencer Enterprises would be okay. We'd be able to carry through with existing projects and new start-ups. But that's not going to happen. We'll be tightening our belts for a while, and that includes your business in the mountain division. I need to see what you've got on the books."

"You want more oversight," Nick said.

"That's right. Everything will have to be evaluated and approved."

Until now, he'd been trying to figure out a way he could work the mine and keep his Spencer Enterprises projects intact. It wasn't going to happen. No way could Nick live with constant supervision.

He circled around his desk. "I'm sure you'll find somebody to handle the mountain division."

Jared's forehead tensed in a frown. "What's that supposed to mean?"

"I've never been a corporate guy. You know it. I know it. Hell, the kid who runs the coffee shop downstairs probably knows it. The only person I really got along with on the management end was Uncle Samuel, and he's gone."

Jared looked at his watch and motioned for

Nick to hurry up. "I know you want something. What are your demands?"

"I have no demands." Nick sat in the chair behind his desk. "I quit."

Jared sat, too. His legs folded under him. "Do you mean that you quit as in take a break?"

"I'm not going to work here anymore."

"What are you going to do?"

"I found out what Samuel was doing in the mountains. He was checking into the feasibility of reopening the Valiant gold mine near Hearthstone. By the way, that was the message he was trying to give us when he died. *Hearthstone* means *heart of stone.* Those were his last words. This was important to him, Jared, and I think I can make it work. In addition to the remaining gold ore in the mine, assay tests show deposits of uranium."

"You sound convinced," Jared said.

"I am."

"You're not taking the money out of Spencer

Enterprises to follow up on this. Do you have another way to pay for it?"

"I do."

His brother massaged his temples with both hands and stared down at the rug. Nick wasn't sure whether Jared would explode in rage or burst into tears. This was an end of an era. Though they'd gone their separate ways in most things, the two brothers had always been on the same team. Jared was the star quarterback, and Nick was always there to catch his passes and make the run into the end zone. Not anymore. Game over.

Jared rose slowly to his feet and held his hand across the desk. "Good luck, Nick."

He shook his brother's hand. "It's not goodbye."

"It better not be. I'm going to need you to babysit my kid."

Nick knew he'd made the right decision. From beyond the grave, Samuel had pushed him into a new life.

# Chapter Twenty-One

*Sunday, 6:00 p.m.*

Kelly knew that Nick was planning to meet his brother, and she kept a wary eye on Jared as he and Lauren came into the class. Jared's mood seemed positive, and she was glad to see him smile while the other couples greeted him and told him that he'd missed a lot.

"It's okay," Lauren announced. "I've been taking notes. I have everything under control."

Her appearance told a different story. Her blond hair flew in frizzy curls around her head, and her clothing was mismatched. Her pregnant waddle was so exaggerated that Kelly marveled that Lauren could make it all the way across the room to sit on the exercise mat. It was obvious that Lauren's baby was coming at any minute.

Roxanne was also making a transition. When she lowered herself onto the exercise mat, she grunted. Every movement she made was accompanied by another groan, but she wasn't voicing her usual sarcastic complaints.

After Kelly got them started with breathing exercises, she knelt beside Roxanne and asked, "Are you uncomfortable?"

"You bet."

"Are you having any cramping?"

"Yeah." She looked up with worry in her eyes. "I've been having these little twitches since this morning. But my water didn't break so I figured I wasn't really in labor."

"After class tonight, I'd like to give you a quick examination to see how close you are."

She crossed the room to Jared and Lauren. Though he hadn't been able to attend any of the other classes, Nick's brother touched his wife with a gentleness that impressed her. Because Jared and Nick had been arguing, she'd thought of him as an adversary. But he shared a lot of similarities with Nick, and that made Kelly like him.

She asked, "Any questions?"

"I'm getting it," Jared said. "The baby has really been running around in there. Does that mean anything?"

"Basketball player," she suggested. "Track star."

"Like his mom." He gave Lauren's hand a squeeze. "I wish I'd been here last week instead of on the other side of the world. You're a champ for putting up with me."

Their genuine warmth touched Kelly's heart. For the first time since she and Nick had burst into his uncle's office and found the old man dying, she felt normal and relaxed. Teaching the Lamaze class fulfilled her. This was how life ought to be.

When she looked through the glass doors

leading into the classroom and saw five men, it took a moment to register their presence. Who were they? Why were they wearing ski masks?

The doors to the classroom swung open.

Kelly leaped to her feet.

The men were carrying guns.

"Stay calm," said the one in front. "We don't want any trouble. We don't want to hurt anybody. Which one of you guys is Jared Spencer?"

Immediately he stood. "I'm right here. I'll do anything you say. Just leave these other people alone."

"You're all coming with me," the leader said, "and you're all going to cooperate."

Jared confronted him. "What do you want?"

"Hostages."

Kelly swallowed hard and tried to think. It was Sunday evening. The downstairs shops were closed, as were the offices. The security men weren't at the front desk. There probably wasn't anyone else in the building, no one to call for help. *No one except Nick.* He had planned to meet his brother in his office before class. Was there some way she could signal him?

She looked toward the wall where her jacket lay crumpled on the floor. Her cell phone was in the pocket.

"And now," the leader said, "we're taking your cell phones."

One of the other masked men circulated among them with a pillowcase, waiting by the men until they handed over their phones. Another went through the women's purses. He found Kelly's cell phone in her jacket.

"Don't get cute," the leader said. "If everything goes the way it's supposed to, we'll be out of here in half an hour."

Roxanne started crying, and the man collecting the cell phones turned on her. "Shut up."

"I can't," she said. "It hurts."

"How can it hurt? I didn't touch you."

"Leave her alone," Kelly said as she stood. "She's going into labor."

*Sunday, 6:18 p.m.*

EVEN THOUGH HE'D QUIT, Nick didn't have to clear out his desk right now. He could probably wait for days or weeks to make that transition, but he wanted to make a final gesture that said he didn't work here anymore.

Using a box from the copy room, he loaded his photos of his kids, a couple of other knick-knacks and the piece of fool's gold that Kelly had found on the floor beside the bookcase. He'd never figured out exactly what it was doing there, and he crossed the room to check out his books and decide if he should take some of them with him now.

The pentagon shape to his office had always bothered him. The slanted closet seemed like a waste of space. He remembered mentioning the weird design to his uncle, who had the office below his with a matching floor plan. Samuel had chuckled and said something cryptic about there always being a reason for design, even if it wasn't apparent.

The obvious reason for Samuel's slanted closet was his hiding place in the back corner. Nick had never checked to see if he had the same design.

He went into the closet, closed the door behind and felt around on the back wall. There was nothing obvious, not a hollow sound when he tapped or a magic knob. Working with his uncle, he'd installed a lot of secret places; Nick knew how this worked. Guided by touch rather than sight, he felt each nail and every irregularity in the design. He was leaving this office for good. If Samuel had added a secret space, he had to find out now or wonder about it forever.

He located the hidden lever and pressed down hard. The wall moved. "I'll be damned."

Instead of a hiding place, he found a pole with rungs on each side—a ladder. Samuel had connected their two offices with another of his secret passages. This provided the explanation for how a killer had gone into his uncle's office and escaped unseen. They climbed up and out.

On the night Samuel died, the only place in the building where the elevator security cameras weren't working was the tenth floor, his floor.

Still inside the closet, Nick heard someone open the door to his office. An unfamiliar voice said, "Where the hell is he?"

Nick stepped onto the ladder and closed the secret panel. He could still hear the men talking.

"He was supposed to be here."

"We've got to find him. We need both brothers to get the gold."

Nick knew what they were talking about. To open the impenetrable bars that protected the Valiant gold, it took two fingerprints simultaneously. Had they already grabbed Jared? Nick silently cursed. His brother had been in Lamaze class with Lauren and Kelly and the other three couples.

When he heard the closet door being yanked open, Nick peeked through a crack in the wood and saw a man in a black ski mask with a gun.

After the gunman rifled through the jackets hanging in the closet, he closed the door.

"He's got to be somewhere in the building."

"Check with Trask. He'll tell us what to do."

Trask? Was the white-haired man running this show?

For a moment Nick considered turning himself over to Trask's men. He didn't want the people in the Lamaze class to suffer while he was hiding out. He decided not to make that move until he had a better idea of the setup. Once he gave himself up, he couldn't change his mind and go back into hiding.

Inside the secret passage—a triangle that was barely wide enough to accommodate Nick's shoulders—he climbed down to his uncle's office. The closet hiding place was in front of the passage, cleverly concealing it. Who else would put a secret panel behind another secret panel but Samuel Spencer? From this hidden corner, he strained to hear what was going on. There seemed to be a lot of people coming and going. He heard a loud scream.

A voice nearer to him, probably in his uncle's office, said, "What's wrong with that broad?"

"She's having a baby. Trust me, she's only going to get louder."

"Can't we shut her up right now? Why do we have to wait?"

"First we get the gold. Then we take care of the hostages."

"Then, ka-bam. No more witnesses."

They meant to kill the hostages. To kill Kelly.

*Sunday, 6:45 p.m.*

KELLY AND HER CLASS had been taken to the conference room outside the vault where the gold was kept. Though she'd pleaded to be able to bring her satchel so she could use the various tools she had to make Roxanne more comfortable, Trask's men refused. This was going to be a miserable labor for all of them.

While the rest of her class sat around the polished conference table, Kelly and Roxanne's husband were with her on the floor in the corner where they tried to make her a cozy nest using jackets. Her labor pains were coming every five minutes, and she was screaming her head off.

Jared approached one of the men in masks. "You said it would only be half an hour. What's the problem?"

"We can't find your brother. We know he's in the building, but we can't locate him."

Roxanne let out another yell.

Another man in a ski mask stalked into the conference room. He had a cell phone to his ear. "I understand. We can't use our explosives. The bars and glass can't be blown without damaging the gold."

Though she had heard that voice only once before, Kelly recognized Trask. He seemed to be taking orders from someone else, someone who wasn't on-site, but he was the boss here and capable of making decisions.

She stood to face him. "We need to get this woman to a hospital. She's in pain."

"She's having a baby," he said. "She'll live."

"But her screams are going to drive you crazy. If you won't let her go, at least move us to a different room where there isn't so much stress."

He nodded to his men. "Take these people into the office on my left, the accountant's office. One of you stay with them so they don't try anything cute. Tear out the phone and shut the damn door so we don't have to hear the noise."

It wasn't much of a concession, but Kelly took it. The more distance between themselves and Trask, the better.

In Marian's office, she helped Roxanne get comfortable on the sofa. If they had been left alone, they might have found things that could be used as weapons, like letter openers or heavy office equipment. But they weren't that lucky.

She noticed one of the husbands crouched beside the chair where his wife was sitting. He had a cell phone—he must have been carrying two of them when Trask's men collected the first batch. When Roxanne screamed again, he had it turned on. Supposedly talking to his wife, he mentioned the ninth floor, hostages and the Spencer Building.

Kelly hoped the police got the message.

*Sunday, 7:13 p.m.*

NICK HAD MOVED FROM the secret passageway to the ventilation system that he'd helped install. These horizontal and vertical ducts formed a maze that went all through the building, providing heat and a swamp cooler system that saved energy in summer. He knew the layout of the system better than anybody else. The most daunting problem was Nick's size. He had to crawl on his elbows through the narrow duct, and it was slow going.

Peeking through ventilation grids, he was able to get a limited vision of what was going on. The center of activity appeared to be the ninth floor where the gold was located. He'd seen explosives being planted in several areas, mostly in the corner offices where a detonation would do the most structural damage.

After he worked his way down to the sixth floor where the sporting-goods distributor was located, he knocked out one of the grids, tearing a good-size hole in the wall, and crawled out. Being free was a tremendous relief, but he didn't take the time to do more than draw a couple of quick breaths.

He ran through the offices. Since the motion sensors turned on overhead lights as he passed, he couldn't keep his presence a secret. He could only hope that he got what he needed before he was found.

Finding a ski mask and a black turtleneck, he dressed to blend in with the other men. He wore jeans instead of black cargo pants, but he wasn't planning to stick around long enough for them to notice. In the back area where products were tested, he found the super crossbow. Armed with this weapon and a dozen steel shafts, he might actually make a difference.

The real problem was disarming the explosives. Remembering how he'd rappelled off the roof, he grabbed the same equipment. They had placed bombs in the corner offices. If he could get down from the roof and break through the windows, he could take care of the bombs.

He heard a police siren approaching the building. He would have been glad to have the assistance if the building hadn't been booby-trapped and the hostages weren't in danger. Taking out his cell phone, he called the number for one of the detectives who had been investigating his uncle's death.

When he answered, Nick was concise. "Detective, there's a hostage situation at the Spencer Building. Four pregnant women, their husbands and a midwife—" Kelly, his darling Kelly "—are being held on the ninth floor."

"I got it," the detective said. "I'm on my way there."

"Don't let them rush the building. The hostage takers have planted explosives and booby traps. I repeat, don't let them rush inside."

"I'll do what I can."

He went to a window and looked down. A swarm of police cars and emergency vehicles had arrived. The Boulder SWAT team would be here at any minute—not that there was anything they could do. The world's best sharpshooter couldn't get an angle to shoot all the way up to the ninth floor.

The officers in uniform were gathering outside the front entrance. Nick wanted to yell down to them to stay out, but even if they heard him, they'd probably open fire.

He watched them coming closer and closer.

And he called the detective again. "There are explosives. For their own safety, the police have to stand down."

"I'm trying," the detective said. "We've got too many jurisdictions here."

Two huge explosions rocked the building. The floor shook. The walls shuddered. Nick held his breath, waiting for the ten-story structure to implode.

# Chapter Twenty-Two

*Sunday, 7:32 p.m.*

The building shuddered and quaked. A scream tore from Kelly's lips. She'd done her best to stay calm, but this was too much. They were all scared, even Jared. She heard other explosions from far away that were less potent than the initial blasts.

Trask stormed into the office. "Who has the cell phone?"

"Nobody," Jared said. "You took them."

"Calling the cops was a bad move. We had to blow the stairwells and all the elevators but one. You just made it harder for yourselves."

Jared tried to negotiate. "Let me talk to the police. I can help you get out of here."

"There's only one way anybody is getting out." Trask shoved a cell phone at him. "Call your damn brother and tell him to come to the ninth floor."

Jared held the phone. "What happens to us after you get the gold?"

"Just get him here."

Kelly couldn't think about what was going to happen next. Her entire focus was consumed by Roxanne, who had abandoned the sofa cushions for the floor. Her screams had subsided into hiccupping sobs. She was ready to push.

Kneeling between her legs, Kelly gave Roxanne instructions, encouraged her to remember the breathing exercises. The rest of the class gathered around them, forming a human shield. One of the men muttered something about this making a hell of a story to tell the kid if they got out of here alive.

They had to get out of there. Kelly wouldn't

let herself believe otherwise. As long as Nick was roaming the building, there was reason to hope.

With a determined effort, Roxanne started to bear down. The baby's head was already crowning.

Roxanne lay back in her husband's arms and groaned. "I can't do it."

"One more time," Kelly said. "One more big push."

It took three more pushes before the baby emerged into Kelly's waiting hands. The tiny infant threw back her arms and wailed. She was perfect. Kelly announced, "She's got a great head of hair."

"Give her to me."

Through her tears, Roxanne gave a weak smile. The hairdresser had just accomplished a tremendous physical feat under the most intense circumstances imaginable. Kelly gave the baby girl to her mother and whispered, "You're a hero."

In just a few moments Roxanne expelled the afterbirth. All things considered, this had been a textbook-perfect birth.

Jared called to Kelly. He had Trask's cell phone. "It's Nick. He wants to talk to you."

She wiped her bloody hands on her jeans as she took the phone. "Roxanne had a baby girl."

"I love you," he said.

It wasn't the best time or the best place, but she still felt the impact of those three little words. Nick didn't make commitments lightly.

Without hesitation, she said, "I love you, too."

"I'm going to get you out of there."

"How can I help?"

"Is Trask working alone?"

As far as she could tell, Trask was still taking orders from the person on the other end of the phone. "I'll ask him."

She stared into Trask's angry eyes, the feature visible through the ski mask. "He wants to talk to your boss, the person you're working for."

"Tell him to come here and open the gates for the gold. That's when I'll tell him."

"Nick is kind of stubborn," she said. "He'd be more cooperative if you released Roxanne and her baby. I'm sure your boss wouldn't mind losing one of the hostages."

"You don't know her," Trask said. Angry, he spewed threats, but Kelly didn't hear his words. He'd said "her." The person he'd been talking to on the other end of the phone was a woman.

To Nick, she said, "He says his boss is determined. She wants the gold."

"A woman," he said. "I understand. Tell Trask to go to the elevators."

Trask grabbed the phone from her and yelled into it.

"He's gone," Kelly said, "but he wants you to go to the elevator."

She desperately hoped that Nick had a plan. Lauren was clutching her belly and groaning. Another baby was on the way.

*Sunday, 8:02 p.m.*

ON THE SIXTH FLOOR Nick shoved the body of a man in black with a ski mask onto the elevator. A steel arrow protruded from the upper left section of his chest. The wound shouldn't be fatal, but Nick didn't care if this man lived or died. His unconscious body was intended as a message for Trask and his men. They weren't getting out of here alive unless the hostages were free.

Nick pushed the elevator button for the ninth floor, then he ran back through the offices of the sporting-goods distributor. There was an inner staircase that communicated with the seventh floor of the distributor. Nick took it. He had more to do.

Trask's boss was a woman, and Nick had a pretty fair idea of who that was. He placed a call to Julia, praying she'd pick up.

"Hello, Nick. I'm sorry that you called me."

"You thought Samuel betrayed you."

"I know he did," she said. Her voice was hard

and bitter, filled with the years of resentment that had driven her to the point of madness.

"You hired Trask to find out what he was doing and he reported back to you," Nick said. "But he was wrong. Samuel wasn't taking trips to Hearthstone to have an affair with Virginia Hancock. They spent the night together as colleagues. She was helping him open the gold mine."

"That wasn't his only betrayal. When I heard the terms of his will, I couldn't let it pass. I was Samuel's wife in every way except the marriage certificate, and he left me with a stipend. I should have inherited it all."

"And that's why you're taking the gold."

"I had to get it before Radcliff made a move next week. You can't negotiate with someone like Barry Radcliff. He'd find a way to take the kilobars." She paused. "You should be thanking me. At least I intend to keep the Spencer treasure intact."

Did she really think she'd get away with this? "The police are already here."

"I know. I'm outside watching."

He had a bad feeling about why she'd want to be close enough to see the Spencer Building. The ultimate revenge against Samuel would be to destroy the ten-story building that had been his greatest success. "I found the ladder that connected my office to Samuel's."

"You should have known it was there. You worked with Samuel often enough to know he loved his little secrets, but this time the joke was on him."

Her hatred for his uncle was darker than he ever would have thought possible. Julia and Samuel had loved each other for years. How did their love become so twisted? "Did you pull the trigger?"

"I should have let Trask do it. He would have been more efficient. I told Samuel I knew about Hearthstone and the gold, and then I shot him."

"And the suicide note? It was his writing."

"I've been signing Samuel's name for years."

All the pieces had fallen into place. His uncle didn't die in a complex scheme to take over the business or a million-dollar loan. He'd been killed by love gone wrong. "Let me help you, Julia. We can still make this turn out all right."

"I think not. I have everything worked out. With plenty of traveling money, I can start a new life. Nobody will be interested in an old lady on a pension. I don't need your help."

"But you need my fingerprint to get the gold." This was his only bargaining chip. "If you let the hostages go, I'll join Trask on the ninth floor. I'll do whatever you want."

"Let's turn that around, shall we? If you go to the ninth floor, I'll release the others."

The lights on the seventh floor went out, and darkness surrounded him. "What the hell is going on?"

"Standard procedure in a hostage situation," she said. "The police have cut the electricity to the building. The stairwells are blocked at the ground floor by the explosions. The elevators aren't running. You're trapped, Nick. Might as well give up."

"Did you ever love him?"

"Too much," she said. "Goodbye, Nick."

He wasn't going to let Julia win, and he sure as hell wouldn't let Kelly die. The thought of losing her was motivation. He wanted a life with her, and he'd do whatever it took to make that happen.

The emergency lights came on.

Crossbow in hand, he made his way to the stairwell.

*Sunday, 9:17 p.m.*

LAUREN'S LABOR WAS far different from Roxanne's lusty yells as each contraction hit. Lauren had struggled gamely for nearly an hour, but she was overcome by fatigue and stress. Lying on the floor, she barely moved. She couldn't even summon the strength for a whimper. Kelly had seen blood when she checked the cervix and suspected internal bleeding.

Lauren needed a doctor. Kelly knew how to perform a C-section and had witnessed several emergency procedures, but she couldn't pull this off by herself on the floor of an office.

In the glow of emergency lights, she looked to Jared. "She needs a doctor. We need to get her to a hospital."

She didn't need to say anything more. He understood the seriousness of the situation. He spoke to the masked man who was watching them. "I need to talk to the man in charge."

"Trask," Kelly said. There was no need to bother pretending. He knew she'd recognized him. "His name is Trask, and we need to talk to him right away."

The masked man stepped out of the office. Though they'd been sequestered here, she had picked up bits and pieces of information. Nick had been on the attack with his crossbow. One of Trask's men was near death, and two others were injured.

When Trask entered the room, Jared didn't waste any time. "My wife needs a doctor. She's dying. My brother won't let that happen. He'll do whatever you say if you let Lauren go."

Trask handed over the phone. "Set it up."

While Jared made arrangements on the cell phone, Kelly tended to his wife. Though fading in and out of consciousness, Lauren managed to squeeze her hand. "We have to save my baby."

"We're going to get you to a hospital. You and the baby are going to be all right."

"I wanted natural childbirth."

"Save your strength."

One of the other women was beside Kelly. "What's going to happen to us?"

"We'll get out of here."

"You can't promise that," her husband said.

Life wasn't about promises or guarantees. The only thing Kelly could offer was hope.

The overhead lights went on, and she blinked in the sudden glare. Something was happening. The situation was about to change.

# Chapter Twenty-Three

*Sunday, 9:32 p.m.*

The negotiations between the police and Trask allowed Kelly to escort Lauren in the elevator to the ground floor, where they would be met by paramedics who would take her to the hospital.

"Then you get back on the elevator," Trask said. "You ride to whatever floor Nick Spencer is hiding on and you pick him up. If I don't see Nick's pretty face when the elevator doors open, I'm going to start by killing the new mother and her baby."

A shudder went through her. "I understand."

With help from the others, Kelly loaded Lauren into the elevator. She was so anxious to get Lauren help that every step seemed to be in slow motion. There might have been something clever that she could plan, but all she cared about was saving Lauren and the baby.

The elevator descended to the ground floor, where she was met by paramedics with a gurney. An officer from SWAT approached her. "You stay here. We'll go back up in the elevator. We can end this now."

"Not without getting all the hostages killed," she said.

"I understand your concerns, miss, but you can't trust hostage takers. Anything you might have negotiated isn't—"

She hadn't gone through hell to be ordered around. Kelly was no longer a doormat, and it was going to take more than a SWAT team to keep her from doing what was necessary.

She pulled the gun from the officer's holster and aimed it at his chest. "Back off. I'm going up, and nobody is going to stop me."

For two seconds of stunned silence, the policeman stood and stared. It was enough time for Kelly to get onto the elevator and toss the gun out before the door closed. There wouldn't be a chance to use it against Trask without endangering others, and she didn't want them to shoot her when they saw a weapon.

On the sixth floor, it stopped.

Nick stood before her. He held open his arms, and she ran to him. While they blocked the elevator door to keep the door from closing, she kissed him for all she was worth. "We have to go."

"Not you," he said. "I'm the one Trask wants. I want you to go into the back of these offices and put your head down."

"What's going to happen?"

"Not much, I hope. I got all the explosives deactivated."

"How do you know about explosives?"

"I worked construction in the mountains. We have to put it in roads and clear the land. I use explosives. Kelly, it doesn't matter how I did it. The bombs are cleared, except for the one in my uncle's office. I had it all set up to rappel down the side of the building, but there wasn't enough time."

"When the bomb goes off, what happens?"

"It's not in the right place to take down the building. There's going to be damage on the ninth floor."

"Where the hostages are," she said.

The elevator dinged madly. "If they keep their heads down, they'll be okay."

She didn't want to take that risk. "Let me come with you."

"I love you, Kelly." He stepped into the elevator. "Stay safe. We'll be together."

She watched the door close.

*Sunday, 9:47 p.m.*

BEFORE THE ELEVATOR DOORS opened, Nick made one last call to the detective he'd been talking to. He'd figured that when the vault was finally opened, Trask and all his men would be standing there watching. That was when the police could make their move. He spoke two words into the phone, "Ten minutes."

"You got it, Nick."

On the ninth floor he faced Trask and four other men. Behind their masks, all he could see was their eyes, but that was enough to know that they all wanted to kill him. He strode past them. "Let's do this."

Trask shoved his shoulder. "You don't give the orders."

"That's Julia's job, right? She's the one who's been telling you to jump and how high. How did that sweet little old lady get you to play by her rules?"

"She's my mother."

"What?"

"Gave me up at birth and kept my younger half brother and half sister. I found her two years ago. We have a lot in common."

"Homicidal tendencies are your family heritage?"

"If you were really as smart as you think, you could have worked it out," he said. "I use the name Y. E. Trask, an anagram for Starkey."

If that wasn't so sick, Nick would have thought it was clever. All along, Julia had been playing them, laughing at them and keeping her secrets.

"Trask. Starkey." Nick shook his head. "Yeah, you're some kind of genius, all right. And how are you planning to get out of here with the gold?"

"We load it in backpacks. And then I take a page from your book." He pointed upward. "A chopper picks us up from the roof."

Nick knew Trask/Starkey's plan would never work; the police already had helicopters in the air. This caper had been doomed to failure as soon as the cops arrived.

"That's not all," Trask said. "I'm setting off explosions in the building as a diversion."

"Clever." But all the bombs were gone, except

one. Nick could only hope that the bomb in his uncle's office wasn't too powerful.

Trask grabbed his arm. "Let's get this gold. I want my payoff."

When he saw his brother, Nick gave him a nod. "The paramedics have Lauren. She's going to be all right."

"That's all I want. For Lauren and our baby to be safe."

Their time for arguing was over. Finally the two brothers were on the same page. Nick hoped the bomb in his uncle's office wouldn't end their relationship in a hellish blaze.

Once again, the lights went out. The electricity to the building had been cut.

*Sunday, 9:57 p.m.*

INSIDE THE OFFICES of the sporting-goods distributor, Kelly decided that she couldn't hide in there when there was something she could do to prevent the hostages from being harmed. Nick said he'd already prepared to rappel down the building to his uncle's office. She'd watched him do just that a few days ago.

There wasn't time for safety equipment. She was good at rock climbing. Her skill would have to be enough. All she had to do was make it to the roof.

The emergency lights provided enough illumination for her to see what she was doing. She dashed into the concrete stairwell and started to climb.

Before she reached the top floor, Trask's men had discovered her. They were in pursuit. She hit the roof and ran to the edge where Nick would have set the equipment to make a descent to his uncle's office. Grasping the ropes, she went over the edge.

She rappelled using the belaying rope. It was different without the harnesses. Her arm strength had to support most of her weight, but she had to go only about twenty-five feet.

Her pursuers were on the rooftop above her, but it didn't sound as if they'd figured out where she had gone. If they spotted her, they could kill her quickly, using their guns. Or they could disable her rope and she'd plummet to her death.

At what point had she decided this was a good plan? Nick loved her and she loved him. She had everything to live for. But living wouldn't be worth much if she let the others die.

Dangling outside the window of Samuel's office, she saw the bomb on his desk. The small, innocent-looking package, which was no bigger than a shoebox, didn't look capable of terrible devastation, but she remembered the earlier explosions that had shaken the ten-story structure.

The window ledge outside the office wasn't wide enough to stand on, but she got a toehold to support herself. Earlier, Nick had felt around the edges, trying to find a lever that would open the window, but he hadn't located any such mechanism. She had to break the glass to get inside, but the noise from smashing through the window would surely draw attention.

Glancing down, she saw lights from the law

enforcement people surrounding the building. The height didn't scare her, but the thought of falling was a very real fear. She had to do something, couldn't just hang here like a fly at the end of a spider's web. Desperately, she pushed against the glass. The window moved.

Apparently, when she and Nick had been experimenting with the window, they hadn't fastened it tightly. While supporting her weight with one arm, she used the fingertips of her other hand to pry at the edge of the casement window. It moved again, only an inch, but it was enough to give her hope.

From the roof, she heard Trask's men. They'd found her. If she didn't move fast, they'd either shoot her or unfasten the belaying rope, causing her to plummet to her death.

She shoved the window open and dove inside.

For the moment, she had survived. But the threat remained. She confronted the package on the desk. The plain box had a couple of wires sticking out and a cell phone attached by duct tape to the top. It didn't look like the kind of bomb she'd seen in movies. There wasn't a red digital clock counting down the seconds until the explosion.

If she threw the bomb out the window, she risked injuring the people below. Was there a way to defuse this thing? In her mind, she heard Nick's voice, soothing her and telling her that she knew the right thing to do. He believed in her. He loved her. It wasn't their time to die.

The stairwell. Other bombs had exploded in the stairwell and hadn't destroyed the building. She needed to get this package to the stairwell, and she had to move fast. The men from the roof would be looking for her.

When she picked up the box, her fingers tingled. She was holding death in her hands. Quickly, she slipped from the office and crept through the cubicles toward the elevator. A strange quiet had fallen over the ninth floor. She peeked over the half wall of a cubicle. The door to the office where her Lamaze class was being held hostage was closed. Two armed men—they had to be the guys who had pursued her across the roof—ran toward Samuel's office.

She kept moving. Though the bomb could be detonated at any instant, it didn't make sense for Trask to set off the explosion while he was nearby. She had time, maybe a few minutes, maybe more. There was no way of knowing.

Nearing the stairwell, she sprinted and flung open the door. Inside, she faced two heavily armed men from the SWAT team.

"This is a bomb." She held up the package. "I don't know what to do with it."

The lead man took the package from her. "You need to get out of here."

Looking down the stairwell, she saw dozens of other men who had climbed over the rubble on the first floor. Trask couldn't stand up to this overwhelming force; he'd have to surrender. A man wearing a vest that said Bomb Squad came forward, took possession of the package and disappeared down the stairs.

"Ma'am," the leader said, "you've got to go."

Kelly had never thought of herself as a particularly brave person. For much of her life, she'd been a doormat. But that had changed. She was in charge of her life and her future.

She stiffened her spine. "I'm not leaving until I know everyone else is safe."

Her attitude must have been convincing because he didn't waste time with objections. While the rest of the SWAT team and police mobilized, she waited near the stairwell with three back-up officers. The stink of prior gunfire and explosions filled the air. Apprehension held her in a tight grasp as she listened for the sound of gunfire. There were only a few pops, but a lot of shouting.

Within minutes—much more quickly than she expected—the confrontation was over. Through the glass doors of the office, she saw the people from her Lamaze class rushing toward her, escorted by the SWAT team. They hugged and laughed and cried, celebrating their escape. What a story they'd have to tell their children!

But the ordeal wasn't over. A knot twisted in Kelly's gut. Where was Nick? When she saw his brother come through the doors, her heart dropped. Why wasn't Nick with him?

She heard the other voices and felt the other hugs, but nothing penetrated her senses until she saw that tall, handsome, commanding man striding toward her. She flew into his arms, determined to never let him go.

*Six months later, Saturday, 1:00 p.m.*

KELLY AND NICK HAD DECIDED to have their September wedding outdoors at Serena's farm. Though they were living full-time in Hearthstone while they got the mining operation going, they were still in a trailer and didn't have a home where their guests could stay and be comfortable. And the Hearthstone Motel had permanent residents who worked at the mine.

Kelly's lacy gown had an empire waist that

concealed her rapidly expanding baby bump, and she felt beautiful as she stood at the front door of the house, looking out at the family and friends who had gathered outside the barn.

Fifi and the other goats weren't causing too much trouble. They'd escaped their pen but were more interested in eating all the flower arrangements than bothering the guests.

Serena, her matron of honor, wrapped her arm around Kelly's waist. "This must mean you're staying in Colorado for good. I wish you lived closer."

"We might make a move. Jared keeps badgering Nick to help out at Spencer Enterprises by doing some designing."

Nick's brother hadn't gotten the Singapore contract, but he'd increased business with dozens of projects closer to home. With Lauren and their healthy baby, he didn't have the heart to travel so much anymore.

Serena asked, "Who's the guy with the gold necklaces?"

"Barry Radcliff, our silent partner in reopening the mine. The tall woman with him was almost on the Olympic team for beach volleyball."

There were a lot of people from Spencer Enterprises that she didn't recognize and many with babies from the Lamaze class. She'd sent an invitation to Arthur and his sister to let them know that she and Nick didn't blame them for what his mother and half brother had done, but they hadn't shown up.

Arthur was probably still bitter. He'd been questioned thoroughly by the police, who suspected a connection with Trask. Nothing had been found to link the two men, other than a DNA similarity. Trask and all his men had given up when confronted by the overwhelming force of SWAT. They were in custody. And Julia had also been apprehended. Her dream of a carefree old age would be lived out in prison.

"Did you ever think things would turn out this way?"

"Are you talking about being held hostage

in a ten-story building? Or opening a gold and uranium mine?"

"I was talking about love, finding your soul mate."

Kelly saw Nick walking through the crowd, shaking hands. Being one of the tallest men around, he was always easy to locate, and she never tired of watching him. In his tuxedo, he was easily the most handsome man she'd ever seen.

"I never expected Nick," she said, "but I deserve him."

\* \* \* \* \*